"How had he been killed?" I heard the tremor in my voice, feeling relieved that this was one corpse I hadn't stumbled upon.

"His head had been bashed in. Brains and blood all over the sheets. Ghastly sight. No one deserves such a dreadful end."

Ben asked, "And the weapon?"

"Elaine's Oscar. The killer had propped it up on the pillow, next to his open wound."

"What then?"

Too Tall Tom was shaking his head. "I can't tell you why—there's no sane explanation, even for a film buff—but I picked up that Oscar and read the inscriptions: 'Best Actress. Elaine Eden. *Bitter Victory*. 1973.' Then the cops came charging through the door, and there I stood, with that goddamn Oscar in my hand . . ."

Enter Dying

Noreen Wald

BERKLEY PRIME CRIME, NEW YORK

This is a work of fiction. Names, characters, places, and incidents either are the product of the author's imagination or are used fictitiously, and any resemblance to actual persons, living or dead, business establishments, events, or locales is entirely coincidental.

ENTER DYING

A Berkley Prime Crime Book / published by arrangement with the author

PRINTING HISTORY
Berkley Prime Crime mass-market edition / September 2002

Copyright © 2002 by Noreen Wald.
Cover art by Jeff Crosby.
Cover design by Jill Boltin.

Visit our website at
www.penguinputnam.com

ISBN: 0-425-18639-3

Berkley Prime Crime Books are published
by The Berkley Publishing Group,
a division of Penguin Putnam Inc.,
375 Hudson Street, New York, New York 10014.
The name BERKLEY PRIME CRIME and the BERKLEY PRIME CRIME
design are trademarks belonging to Penguin Putnam Inc.

PRINTED IN THE UNITED STATES OF AMERICA

10 9 8 7 6 5 4 3 2 1

To Susan Kavanagh, with gratitude
and to the memory of Mary Fahy Celeste

Acknowledgments

Susan Kavanagh, niece, friend, and editor, I couldn't have done it without you!

Diane Dufour, Barbara Giorgio, Doris Holland, Gloria Rothstein, Pat Sanders, and Joyce Sweeney, thanks for listening.

Thanks to my son, Billy Reckdenwald, for his expert advice on navigating the streets of New York City.

Finally, thanks to my editor, Tom Colgan, and my agent, Peter Rubie.

One

"Greige," my mother said. "So perfect for fall, don't you think?"

"What?" the bridal consultant asked, entering the dressing room, her arms filled with yards of taupe silk. No doubt yet another prospect for my maid of honor gig.

"Jake's gown! Isn't greige great?" Mom asked the harried but beaming consultant, who nodded, smiled even wider—exposing lots of white teeth—then eagerly agreed.

Why shouldn't Sally the Sales Shark be happy? Closing in on her prey, smelling a big kill, savoring a hefty commission. For God's sake, this number sported an eight hundred dollar price tag.

I knew from greige . . . a combination of gray and beige. After all, I'd grown up surrounded by neutrals. The only baby girl in Queens dressed in head-to-toe ecru. And I knew that Maura O'Hara's wedding gown and the dresses worn by her maid and matron of honor would be every bit as colorful as her ivory-to-cream wardrobe and her cream-to-caramel decor.

"I'd call that pewter," Gypsy Rose Liebowitz, our old

family friend, New York's favorite fortune-teller, and Mom's matron of honor, said as she adjusted the folds in the full skirt of the taffeta gown that I couldn't zip up. In my unspoken opinion, the color in question looked more like three-day-old cigarette ashes.

We were all standing in Bergdorf Goodman's Bridal Salon—in a dressing room larger than many Manhattan studio apartments—staring at my reflection in a floor-to-ceiling mirror. So far, I hadn't said a word. No one had seemed to notice.

"Pewter?" Mom's eyebrows scrunched together and her voice took on a testy tone. "Gypsy Rose, do you mean to tell me that you see more gray than beige in Jake's dress? Won't that clash with the champagne tones in my wedding gown?"

I sighed and reached for the taupe silk.

"You'll love this one," Sally the Sales Shark gushed. "No conflicting undertones. Like caviar, taupe is destined to go with champagne!"

Since my checkered childhood, when Mom had inherited our co-op on Ninety-second Street from her great-aunt, we'd lived on Mom's income from copyediting, working part time in Gypsy Rose's New Age bookstore, and creative credit card juggling. Then, after I'd become a ghostwriter, my income helped to cover the monthly maintenance fee. And, recently, more than just the basics. So I've remained a ghost.

Through the years, I've tolerated Tiffany because of its proximity to FAO Schwarz and, as I grew older, because of the Truman Capote–Audrey Hepburn connection, but Mom's never-ending romance with Bloomingdale's and Bergdorf's—mostly during their sales—has sent me shopping at Loehmann's. Amid all this Fifth Avenue elegance and prewedding excitement, I would have preferred to be there right now.

A week from today, my mother would be marrying my on-again/currently very much off-again boyfriend's father. The groom, Aaron Rubin, a tall, slim, gray-haired, living, breathing, walking, talking Ralph Lauren ad patriarch, had recently been elected the junior senator from New York, following his predecessor's demise. A messy murder case that his son, Ben, an NYPD homicide chief, and I had helped solve. Though not working side by side. Whenever I played detective, Ben considered me a big-time pain.

Despite our unresolved issues, next Friday evening at St. Thomas More Church in our Carnegie Hill parish, Ben will serve as his father's best man and I will be my mother's maid of honor.

Complicating all this cozy intrigue, Dennis Kim, New York City's top entertainment attorney and my other on-again/off-again boyfriend—our relationship has remained in a constant state of flux since I was eight and he was twelve—will usher. And his *father*, Mr. Kim, another dear old family friend, as well as our local greengrocer, will give the bride away.

"Jake, come back from wherever you are," Mom said, "and take a look in the mirror!"

Shaking off wedding day woes, I obeyed my mother.

Totally amazing! After eight weeks, seven stores—starting and ending in Bergdorf—and thirty-six rejects, I'd put on a dress that was love at first sight. Based on the enthusiasm in Mom's voice, the glint in Gypsy Rose's eyes, and the satisfied smirk on the bridal consultant's face, I gathered they all loved it as much as I did.

The object of our mutual admiration was a silk shantung sheath with a Sabrina neckline and a bell-shaped skirt that slimmed my hips and flattered my waist. Taupe and terrific!

Gypsy Rose laughed. "Jake, I'd just about accepted that you'd walk down the aisle in one of your Annie Hall pantsuits. Complete with that god-awful tie you've been wearing since your thirteenth birthday!"

She and my mother had picked out and been fitted for their outfits two months ago. Right in this very dressing room. Mom immediately renounced ice cream and Milky Ways until after the wedding reception. Her soft silk champagne gown and matching tiny silk tiara reminded me of Empress Josephine's style. While Gypsy Rose's elaborate café au lait gown could have come straight from the court of Marie Antoinette. Vera Wang with a French twist.

Sally the Sales Shark sailed off to find the seamstress, pausing long enough to deliver a dramatic exit line: "The poor dear will have to work double time to get you ready, Jake!"

I waved the price tag in her wake. "At nine hundred and fifty dollars, I hope the alterations are included!" She never veered from her course.

Actually, I shouldn't have been complaining. As a wedding present to Mom, Gypsy Rose, the most generous woman I know, had insisted on paying for all three of our dresses.

· · · · ·

Two hours later, Mom, Gypsy Rose, and I celebrated with tea and huge blueberry muffins in Sarabeth's Kitchen. Crossing off another item—*get Jake's dress*—on our long list of premarital tasks.

The restaurant, located in the Wales Hotel on Madison Avenue, around the corner from our co-op, has been part of my life and its small successes since shortly after Mom and I had moved to Carnegie Hill from Jackson Heights, twenty-six years ago.

As has Gypsy Rose Liebowitz. A good-looking redhead, with fashion flair as wild as her curls, an untamed curvy figure, and great legs, she's now a senior citizen, with a child's sense of exploration. And expectation. Her remarkably youthful spirit, depth of soul, wicked wit, and worldly wisdom have brought grace and color into our lives. Not even Mom can live on beige alone. Since Gypsy Rose was a widow with no children, I've been the lucky recipient of her loving nature. Mom and I adore her.

Though sometimes her psychic connections both puzzle

and alarm me. An evening at Gypsy Rose's can include guests from the world beyond. Zelda Fitzgerald and Emily Brontë have shown up. Zelda, on occasion, brings a message from Jack O'Hara, my late father. Even George Sand made a cameo appearance. I remain a skeptic, but can't explain what the hell happens when Gypsy Rose channels the spirit world. I do believe that Gypsy Rose believes. And way beyond belief, communications from these long-dead writers have helped me catch killers. As Sister Mary Agnes told me in the third grade: "Life's a mystery!" Apparently death is, too!

As if reading my mind, Gypsy Rose gave me an impish grin and said, "Jake, darling, I want you to know Zelda tells me your father approves of your mother's upcoming marriage."

I swallowed the last bite of my muffin, then said, "Oh?"

Mom, the intrepid chatterbox, kept quiet. We both stared at Gypsy Rose, waiting.

"Yes." Gypsy Rose smiled. "Zelda showed up rather inconveniently, last night while I was waiting for a soufflé to rise. She'd been playing Hearts with Jack. As usual, he'd won. Anyway, Zelda knew the wedding was on my mind, and had asked Jack how he felt about it. He'd wished Maura happiness and long life. Said he'd be the one waltzing her around eternity, but he didn't mind Aaron cutting in."

While I found my dead father's *answer* to be somewhat ambiguous, my mother smiled and sounded relieved. "Isn't that wonderful, Jake?"

Mom and Dad had been long divorced before his untimely move to the world beyond. Upon his death, Mom assumed the mantle of widowhood—both she and Gypsy Rose had totally overdosed on Jackie Kennedy— and canonized my father's memory.

"Just great!" What else could I say?

"Well, after Jack Kennedy died," Mom pressed on, "Jackie married Ari. Now that they've all gone to the world beyond, I'm sure they've worked out . . ."

Elizabeth Taylor's eight marriages crossed my mind. Fortunately, my cell phone rang before I could speak.

"Jake!"

"Hi, Dennis."

"Where are you? I need to see you right now. Can you grab a cab down to my office?"

Mom's frown sent me outdoors.

I stood on the corner of Ninety-second and Madison, the wind whipping autumn leaves over my brown boots and blowing ash blonde hair into my eyes. And memories clouding my mind. Memories of Venice in June, Dennis and I walking across the Bridge of Sighs, where he'd proposed for the third and last time. Still feeling his lips on my cheek. Still wondering why I hadn't said yes.

"What's so urgent, Dennis? I'm celebrating at Sarabeth's with Mom and Gypsy Rose. I finally found a dress for the wedding—"

"Jake, you do know that Sir Gareth Selby-Steed's coproducing *Suzy Q?*"

"Of course I know!" Hadn't I ghosted Kate Lloyd Connor's *A Killing in Katmandu*, the novel the musical had been based on? Hadn't Dennis invited me to attend *Suzy Q*'s opening night? Selby-Steed was one of his biggest clients. Why did Dennis sound so frazzled? Very out of character.

"The show's in big trouble, Jake. The leading lady's about to walk. The music's marvelous, but the dialogue's deadly. Gareth needs a ghostwriter to prop up the lines. Get some life into them. Quick. The show opens Thursday night!"

"You can't be thinking of me, can you? Mom's getting married on Friday!"

"Jake, you'll remain anonymous, but the pay is astronomical. You'll breeze through this assignment."

"Get another ghost. I'm too busy being the bride's maid of honor. Every night from now to the wedding is booked. The rehearsal. Gypsy Rose's party. Your own dinner party for Mom at—"

"Come on, if you pull this off, you can retire on the royalties."

"I've heard that song before."

"But wouldn't you just die if you passed up this opportunity to work with Elaine Eden?" Dennis actually sounded desperate. "It could be the lady's last hurrah."

The truth was—and he damn well knew it—Mom would be the one who'd *die* and want to kill me, too, if I refused Dennis Kim's offer.

TWO

Forty years ago, Mom had been first runner-up in the annual Miss Rheingold contest. The winner had been Maria Elena Buttofuco, who'd taken her prize money, moved from Rego Park to Greenwich Village, enrolled in the American Academy of Dramatic Arts, and morphed into Elaine Eden. Broadway star. A household name— even in the hinterlands. In the early 1970s, the Tony Award–winning stage actress whose only screen role had put an Oscar on her mantel, recorded a country album and won a Grammy!

Maura Foley, on the other hand, had received several cases of Rheingold beer, married Jack O'Hara, and eventually produced me. Some consolation prize.

My childhood bedtime stories included an ongoing series of news bulletins about Elaine Eden's life. Far more entertaining than Mother Goose. The theater's first lady had accumulated six Tonys and had married seven times. Her only son, fathered by her first husband, would be about my age. Last I'd heard, he'd been living in a monastery in Tibet.

Since their shared spotlight all those decades ago,

Elaine had neither returned Mom's calls, nor sent her as much as a Christmas card. Yet that star power still pulled my mother, albeit vicariously, into Eden's life.

When I returned to the table, Mom egged me on. "What a marvelous opportunity, darling! Since you wrote the original manuscript, you're the perfect book doctor to cure what ails *Suzy Q!*" Giggling like a schoolgirl, she added, "Then we can all go to opening night."

Gypsy Rose seconded her opinion.

I called Dennis back, accepted his offer, and negotiated for him to drive over to Sarabeth's and pick me up.

After he'd sweet-talked Mom and Gypsy Rose, pocketed a muffin for the road, and paid our check, my mother issued a final request. "Please have Jake back by seven, Dennis. Tonight's the last literary salon I'll be hosting as Maura O'Hara. I don't want either of you to miss it!"

The lesser literary lights of Carnegie Hill gathered once a month at Mom's. The membership had topped out at thirty. Mostly unpublished writers—though every once in a while some obscure literary journal would "buy" one of their stories, paying them with free copies. Mr. Kim, Dennis's dad, was a charter member and the group's resident poet. In our neighborhood, his odes were as much admired as his produce.

Pointing to her long list of things yet to be done, I said, "I thought you might cancel tonight's meeting, Mom."

"Cancel?" She sounded appalled. "Never! Why, since this is such a special occasion, Gypsy Rose is channeling Erle Stanley Gardner as our ghost guest of honor. Don't miss this, Jake. You might learn something!"

I couldn't quibble with that.

. . . . .

Ten minutes later, Dennis and I sat in his Rolls-Royce en route to the Waldorf-Astoria to meet with *Suzy Q*'s music man and coproducer.

Two years ago, the newly knighted Brit had taken America by storm with his rock opera, *Lady Godiva's*

Hair. Last year, his gaudy—some said tasteless—show, *Catherine the Great's Horse*, won the Tony for best musical. Sir Gareth Selby-Steed must have a thing for jockeys.

Dennis, still sweet-talking, said, "Just think, Jake, you'll be rewriting the words for a show with the great Gareth's music! What better billing could a fledgling playwright want?"

"Have you switched from entertainment law to fiction writing, Dennis? You, of all people, know a ghost gets no credit!"

"Listen, credited or not, *Suzy Q* needs a fast rewrite and a dose of Jake O'Hara's snappy dialogue. With the opening only days away, the producer's willing to pay big bucks for a little wit." Dennis talked money, knowing that would be the direct route to my inspiration.

Though I'd never admit it to either Mom or Dennis, I, too, thought this would be an exciting project. The musical had caught Broadway's fickle fancy. And its players were the tabloids' current darlings. The casting question had rivaled the search for Scarlett. Every over-the-hill Broadway and Hollywood actress auditioned to star as Suzy Q. After all, how many starring roles were there for sixty-something-year-old actresses?

But the role had gone to Elaine, who possessed all the necessary accouterments. The lady could sing, dance, act, and, currently, was sleeping with the show's director, Philip Knight.

Dennis pulled into a no-parking zone on Lexington and Fifty-first, and we walked down a block to the Waldorf. I love the lobby. Stretching east from Lexington to Park, and north from Forty-ninth to Fiftieth, the hotel's vast space, through some marvelous decorating skills and clever placement of furniture, offers its guests an aura of gracious, timeless living.

"Where are we meeting Sir Gareth?" I asked as Dennis exited the revolving door.

"The Bull and the Bear," he said, leading me to the

restaurant's crowded bar. Lots of wood and brass. Lots of men. I could count the women on one hand. Five-thirty P.M. The "masters of the universe" were holding court. The markets had posted their final numbers. The ad agencies had drafted their final copy. The senior NBC News staff—some of whom actually had worked there since the days of Huntley and Brinkley—knew when to take a martini break. And the bankers, who always beat the other professions to the bar, had been perched on their favorite stools for at least an hour. Interspersed with the gray hair and gray three-piece suits were the young lions in navy blazers and chinos. The few women wore black.

But no sign of Gareth.

I asked Dennis, "Isn't this atmosphere a tad clubby and conservative for a man who moves to the sound of a different orchestra?"

"Hello! Over here!" I swung around. Selby-Steed and entourage had arrived, in all their glitzy glory.

In person, Gareth's head loomed even larger than it did on television or in photographs. Very short, about five two max, his round face, with its massive rosy cheeks and Dutch Boy blonde bob, seemed to take up a third of the small space that Mother Nature had allotted him. He wore a tight-fitting burgundy leather zippered jacket, and appeared much younger than his admitted forty-five years. Selby-Steed's loud, audacious entrance had the mostly conservative crowd whispering, pointing, and peering over their Cosmopolitans. Some even applauded.

Trailing behind him, in the Prince Philip mode requisite distance, came an odd trio. The first, a pale young woman with spiky chestnut brown hair, dressed in a Mary Quant retro mini and ankle-high white boots. The second, a tall, painfully thin man, wearing skin-tight black leather pants and a jeans jacket. And the third, a fat, older man with a dour face, sporting a two thousand dollar suit that couldn't quite cover his girth, and brandishing a huge, unlighted cigar as if it were a weapon in his right hand. A pinkie ring, with a ruby the size and color of his wide, flat nose, weighed down his left hand. Though not nearly as short as Selby-Steed, the fat man had elevator heels on his alligator boots. I couldn't dredge up his name, but I recognized this Runyonesque character as *Suzy Q*'s other major investor. Mucho money. Reported mob connections. And a face you couldn't forget.

Not bothering to introduce any of them or allowing Dennis—who did try—to introduce me, Gareth said, "Come, follow me, I've reserved a table down front."

We followed. A waiter led us to a window table.

As dusk settled over the city, hordes of people passed by. Office workers rushing toward the subway, shoppers, looking wearier than the workers, waiting for a downtown bus, and twenty-somethings dashing out for drinks and dinner, hailing cabs.

Without consulting us, Gareth ordered champagne and caviar for everyone. Then he finally got around to introducing his companions. "The bird on my right is Cynthia Malone. Best seamstress since Betsy Ross during that unpleasant episode when the colonies rebelled against Mother England."

I hated him midsentence.

Dennis squeezed my knee, signaling me not to jump all over our host.

Gareth Selby-Steed rolled right on. "In addition to overseeing our costumes, poor dear Cyn is stuck pro tem as Elaine's dresser. The last one committed suicide, didn't she, luv?"

"That's right. Slit her wrists." Cynthia Malone's voice surprised me. I'd expected a British accent. "After two weeks of zipping up Elaine Eden, I can understand why!"

Interesting. Just as I'd detested the composer almost as soon as he opened his mouth, I instantly liked Cynthia.

"And this," Selby-Steed said, "is my coproducer, Auturo Como. Of course, he needs no introduction."

Auturo smiled. And went from dour to dimpled as he showed off his small well-capped teeth. A mouthful of money. "Jake O'Hara, I am most honored to meet you.

Dennis Kim has assured me that you are the woman who will save our show!"

Smiling back, I nodded but said nothing.

Humph! Dennis must have been *pretty* positive that I'd accept his offer. Way too positive!

"Last and certainly least." Gareth chuckled, then pointed to the tall, thin man, sitting to his left. "This bloke is Larry Cotter, who wrote the bloody book for this bloody musical mess. The only reason he hasn't been fired straightaway is that you're a ghostwriter. Someone has to receive credit for the script in the playbill, might as well be Larry, don't you think?"

Before I could tell Sir Selby-Steed just what I did think, he roared, "And Larry's my bloody boyfriend, isn't he? Now I ask you, Jake, how do you get rid of a lover?"

Damned if I knew.

Three

"I'm mad about the boy, but the lad has no ear for music. And his words have desecrated my arrangements!" Gareth Selby-Steed said.

After gulping his caviar and champagne, Larry, the *boy* to whom the composer referred, had discreetly disappeared right on cue, taking Cynthia Malone with him.

Now Gareth and Auturo the Angel—as a New York gossip columnist had dubbed the rotund producer decades ago—were getting down to business.

Como grimaced. Dimples gone. Dour puss back in place. "Madness might explain why you hired that wimp to collaborate with you. The man had never written a book for a musical, yet you financed your lover's debut with my money!" Then the angry angel turned to me. "Sir Selby-Steed's magic couldn't carry *Suzy Q*. We could have won a Tony. But our besotted knight, here, let that talentless twit muck up my musical!"

Selby-Steed pounded on the table, drawing frowns from the people sitting near us. "*Your* musical? Why you bloody oversized baboon! I have half a mind to take my

score and fly straightaway to London! Let you lose your
millions of pounds—"

"Half a mind is half again more than what you have!"
The producer's Jell-O jowls shook.

"Gentlemen, please," Dennis said.

Jeez! Working with these two guys would be worse
than working with the former Queen of Murder Most
Cozy, the late Kate Lloyd Connors. Here I thought I'd
left *A Killing in Katmandu* and its heroine in the dust. Did
I really want to ghost script the same story? Though that
would have to be a first. But I'd have all these magna
cum loud egos vetting my every word!

"Sorry, Dennis," Gareth said, almost as if he meant it.
Then he turned to me, taking my hand in his. I've never
felt such soft skin. Not even Mom's, which she always
kept swathed in Vaseline Intensive Care. "Jake, don't allow our petty bickering to dissuade you. I stayed up all
night reading *A Killing in Katmandu*. And I know you—
er—edited Ms. Connors's manuscript. An excellent job,
my dear. I'm sure you can save our play. Infuse *Suzy Q*
with the same brand of lively dialogue that made the novel
such a joy!"

He'd done his homework. Since we ghosts never take
credit for any books we've written, "editing" has become
an accepted code word for what we really do.

I met Gareth's gaze, but said nothing. His smooth hand
held my much rougher one in a viselike grip. "Larry tried,
but how can you expect a British lad to step into the mind
and heart of a character as complex and as American as
Suzy Q?"

Love is really blind! Larry Cotter had to be in his mid-
forties. He hadn't been a lad since the early 1970s.

Auturo snarled, "Elaine Eden can't step into character,
either. That old broad plays every role as if she's reprising
her moment of glory as Regina in *The Little Foxes*."

"You can't blame me for casting that tone-deaf cow!
Philip Knight's besotted with her," Selby-Steed said.
"Only God knows why. As you bloody well know, he

wouldn't direct the goddamn show without your former paramour as star. What do you straight old Broadway guys do, pass the has-beens around like hors d'oeuvres?"

Auturo turned scarlet—with all that extra weight, I hoped he wouldn't have a stroke—then screamed, "That woman lost her box office pull years ago. She turned my last show, what should have been a hot ticket, into a cold turkey. I'd only signed her on as a favor for a friend— yet another starstruck angel. Do you know where that favor got me? Six million smackers in the hole! That's where!" He pulled out a silk handkerchief and wiped the sweat off his upper lip. "And I haven't slept with that broad since she was a size six—back when you were still in nappies, Gareth. If Philip Knight hadn't brought some really big money on board with him, I wouldn't have given that bitch a walk-on!"

As I squirmed, attempting to extricate my fingers from Gareth's clenched fist, Dennis said, "Gentlemen, let's not get off track. We all know Jake's your last chance to salvage this mess, and she's used to working with difficult women. In fact, it's her stock-in-trade. She's literally cornered the market. So let's move on. We'll require a percentage of the gross as well as a consultation fee. Not being credited demands both an excellent advance and ongoing royalties."

· · · · ·

Fifteen minutes later, we'd signed the contract. I would report to work at ten tomorrow, after reading the script tonight. Despite my severe reservations, I felt giddy—high on greed and glee. Doctoring *Suzy Q*'s script might turn me into a rich woman!

With almost an hour to spare before Mom's literary salon began, Dennis suggested that we have a drink in the lobby.

We sat on a love seat, closer together than necessary, sipping champagne cocktails, chatting about the assignment, mapping strategy, rather than talking about us.

Dennis said, "Can this Elaine Eden be as big a bitch as Como and Selby-Steed say she is?"

"Her track record would indicate so. As you've heard a hundred times, Mom placed second in a long-ago Miss Rheingold contest that started Elaine on her career, and I'd bet I've been exposed to more of Eden's sordid exploits than even her most fanatic fans."

"Other than winning some acting awards—ages ago— and getting married and remarried, what has Elaine done lately?"

"Jeez, Dennis! Don't you ever read *Variety*? I'd think that as an entertainment attorney, that would be your bible."

"Well, she's something of a relic, isn't she? Doesn't get much coverage these days. I did read an article last week about what a femme fatale she'd once been. But, Jake, that's ancient history, right?"

"Well, her current boyfriend, Philip Knight, is still legally married, but that never stopped Elaine. In the mid- to late sixties, she shocked the world! Set—or lowered, depending on one's attitude—the standard for sexual shenanigans. Had several well-publicized affairs with married men, stealing a husband or two from clueless wives in an era when that kind of behavior should have totally killed her career."

"Why didn't it?"

"Because, as Mom, *People* magazine, and Liz Smith all agree, for over forty years, Elaine Eden has been the star we love to hate. Her immorality makes us feel good."

"Has your mother ever heard from her?"

"No. Not since the beauty contest. But not for lack of trying. Elaine never returned Mom's phone calls and, apparently, never read her fan letters, either."

"So, not a nice lady."

I hummed a few bars of "The Lady Is a Tramp." Off key. Probably to shut me up, Dennis asked the piano player to play "As Time Goes By."

Then we both sang along, not missing a word of my favorite song,

Being this close to Dennis activated the twitch that has teased me for over a quarter of a century—warming my heart as it spread from my throat to my toes.

He kissed me, a light touch that lingered, promising more, and said, "If you married me, you could stop being a ghost and finish that potential Pulitzer Prize–winning novel, couldn't you?"

I started. Dennis's first romantic words since we'd left Venice! What had sparked them? Why question? Right now I wanted to hear them. Even though my mother was about to marry my former boyfriend's father. Great! Mom will be Mrs. Rubin. I'll be Mrs. Kim. And Ben? How would he feel? I'd hurt him—a lot—when I'd gone off to Venice with Dennis. And Ben and I hadn't really talked since I'd returned . . . still single.

I glanced across the lobby. Then squinted. No question about it, I need glasses. But wasn't that Ben? With an arm draped around the shoulder of that leggy brunette detective? Sandy Ellis. A cool, calculating woman with the best haircut in Manhattan. . . . Who wears designer suits on homicide calls.

As Dennis's baritone boomed, *"These fundamental things apply,"* I stared at Ben.

Of all the hotel bars in all the lobbies in all of New York City, he had to walk into . . . God . . . though our roles were reversed . . . this was so *Casablanca*!

Four

"Yes, can you believe my fourth husband was the nineteenth son in a family of fifty-two children? Different mamas, you understand, but one papa. Quite a guy. A Saudi billionaire. Oil. But Faid suffered from a severe case of sibling rivalry syndrome. The problems started during our honeymoon in the South of France. He had these ghastly nightmares, and would wake up swinging, thinking that I was one of his sisters. Though I hated to fail yet again, his wild attacks in the middle of the night made our marriage impossible. But when the sun shone and in the shank of the evening, Faid was quite a guy, himself. *Quel dommage!*"

Dennis and I stared at each other, then started to laugh. We'd arrived at Mom's party to find Elaine Eden center stage, holding her audience rapt.

My mother caught my eye and waved us over to her side.

"Jake, look who's come to see you! My former fellow contestant Elaine Eden!"

The star turned and flashed even better dental work than Auturo's at me. Her smile seemed a tad tight—three face-lifts will do that—otherwise, she looked like the glamour girl she'd been for well over forty years.

As Gareth had, Elaine seemed much smaller in person. Her famous hourglass figure had shifted, now thick in the middle and bottom heavy, but her posture remained perfect. She hadn't changed a hair in her sleek platinum coif since she'd stolen the style from Lana Turner circa *Madame X*. And her makeup, featuring full 1950s Technicolor, was so retro, it was in again. In her aquamarine silk dinner suit—the exact shade of her eyes—she could have been heading to the Stork Club, if it hadn't been closed for decades.

"Jake O'Hara! So good to meet you! I didn't want to crash your mother's party, but she insisted that I stay."

I'll bet.

"Anyway, it's you I really want to talk to. Auturo called me with the happy news . . . and I do want to assure you that you'll have my complete cooperation."

"Thank you, Miss Eden. I'm glad—"

"However, my dear, there are one or two tiny, truly teeny suggestions I'd like to make before you get started. Now, can we go off to some wee corner and have a little chat?"

Amazing how she'd squeezed all those synonyms for *small* into a couple of sentences.

"And do call me Elaine. After all, your mother and I are old acquaintances. Right, Maura?"

I watched Mom's face fall—metaphorically—down to her fanny. Elaine sounded like a royal pain in the butt. Would I ever get to ghost for a normal person? My career path has been cluttered with wicked witches. This smelled like déjà vu all over again. And where had Dennis gone? Was he deliberately avoiding Elaine?

I led the star to a window bench that, in the daylight, offered a great view of Ninety-second Street, and settled in. After a dozen years as a ghostwriter, I'd become a *really* good listener.

Elaine wasted no time. "Jake, please take no offense.

I'm aware that you helped Kate Lloyd Conners with the *Killing in Katmandu* manuscript, but I find that its main character—*my* character—Suzy Q lacks oomph. And I can't blame that idiot playwright Larry, much as I'd love to. You see, Jake, I've read the novel. No oomph there, either!"

"Oomph?"

"Yes! And my audience expects—deserves—oomph! Suzy Q is much too bland to be portrayed by Elaine Eden!"

"Bland?" I felt fury cover me like an itchy blanket. How could this broad . . .

"Colorless. Elaine Eden can't play a colorless character."

Damn! I hated it when people referred to themselves in the third person.

"For God's sake, Suzy Q is a cross between Jackie Kennedy after Camelot and Diana Rigg as Emma Peel! How can you think she's bland?"

"Well." Elaine frowned, making her look older and meaner. "All that world's most famous woman turns into an Avenger stuff is acceptable, if not terribly exciting—but I'm talking about Suzy Q's personal life. It lacks sparkle."

"Sparkle?" Why did I keep repeating every criticism she made? "She's in Katmandu. Exotic locale. Embassy parties. International intrigue—"

"Yes, but Jake, the sex is less than sensational."

"Suzy Q is, as you are . . ."—I'd started to say a senior citizen, but did some fast editing—"an older woman."

Elaine stood. "My fans, like me, are women of a certain age. While their sex life may not sizzle, they expect mine to. And so do I. Suzy Q lacks passion. Think *Sex and the City*!"

I pictured Sarah Jessica Parker in an Assisted Living residence, and started to giggle.

Elaine glared at me. "My car is waiting." She spun around, then looked back over her shoulder. "You are aware that my contract gives me script approval, aren't you? I suggest you start rewriting my character. See you tomorrow."

Gypsy Rose, carrying a small tray, appeared on the scene. Hearing Elaine's exit line, she winked at me, then offered me a choice of Diet Coke or white wine.

"I'll have the Coke, thanks. Looks like I'll be working till the wee hours!"

"Your mother's idol has feet of clay and a heart of stone, I'd say." Gypsy Rose sat down next to me on the window seat. "Elaine Eden's one mean old broad. Have you ever noticed, Jake, that most women who age well become more tolerant? Warmer. Caring more about people and espousing causes. Sharing their wisdom and their wit. Growing more charming, if you will. Others turn into Medusa. And I think it's a conscious choice."

"Why would anyone choose to be a miserable bitch?"

"Some, I believe, are born like that—very few, thank God. As for Elaine, I'd say she grew into the role. Thinks it's an attention getter. Makes her feel she's as important—as noticed—as she'd been when she was young and beautiful."

"Well, I think she was born a bitch."

. . . . .

In the morning, I leaped out of bed, hopped in the shower, and beat Mom into the kitchen, knowing that if I made breakfast, the bagels would have a fighting chance of not ending up burnt.

I'd read, scribbled, and deleted all references to the heroine's age—adding as much sex, passion, sparkle, and oomph as I could muster in the middle of the night, to Suzy Q's character. I rewrote till 2:30 in the goddamn morning, then fell asleep. I found the script stuck under my pillow when the alarm went off at 7:30.

"Darling, you shouldn't be making breakfast." Mom rubbed her eyes, then stretched her arms over her head. Even in her old terry bathrobe and fuzzy mules, my mother looked pretty cute for a woman two years away from Social Security. "After Friday, you'll be on your own!" I thought she was about to cry, but she forged on. "So this is my last chance to spoil you—at least until I return from my honeymoon."

I didn't want to go there. Though Mom and I had agreed that our living arrangements would have to change once she and Aaron were married, we disagreed—big time—on *how* they'd change.

As a senator, Aaron would need to spend a good deal of his time in Washington. He'd bought a great apartment in the Westchester, an elegant old art deco building in the Northwest section of DC, near the National Cathedral, but he and Mom wanted to keep our co-op on Ninety-second Street, too. And they didn't want me to move, stressing that "we'll be gone more a great deal of the time, Jake!"

While that might be true, I knew Maura O'Hara. She'd be showing up any Wednesday to stand in line at Duffy Square to purchase half-price tickets for her beloved Broadway matinees. This woman, a born and bred New Yorker, would be flying back and forth on the shuttle between Reagan National and LaGuardia as if she were riding on the IRT.

And that might be okay, but she'd drag Aaron with her, and he'd be a newlywed with a stepdaughter draped around his neck like an albatross.

Try as I would, I couldn't convince either of them that three's a crowd. So now they were bidding on the second-floor apartment, directly above ours, the goal being to turn the two apartments into a duplex, with me living upstairs. Knowing I wanted to be independent, they suggested that, since I paid our co-op fee each month, I could also pay my share of the duplex's monthly costs.

I'd asked them what part of *no* they didn't understand. They told me the word wasn't in their vocabulary. For now, I've given up the fight. Fortunately or unfortunately, depending on one's point of view, the apartment upstairs hasn't become available yet, and I'd been working on finding my own place. I discovered that a studio in Carnegie Hill rents for $3,500 a month. And the truth was, since I don't want to leave the neighborhood, Aaron's duplex offer was beginning to sound better and better.

Mom and I had a good gossip about last night's lesser literary lights gathering and concurred that Elaine Eden's next award should be for Biggest Bitch in the Universe.

Leaving the co-op, I had a major resentment, because I wouldn't be able to attend my Ghostwriters Anonymous meeting at the Jan Hus church. A couple of years ago, a small group of us New York City ghosts had formed a support group, to work a twelve-step program to help us cope with our anonymity. We now numbered thirty. I certainly could have used a dose of serenity this Saturday morning. How I'd love to share this goddamn ghost story with my three best friends and fellow members of Ghostwriters Anonymous, Too Tall Tom, Modesty, and Jane.

But the theater beckoned.

I decided to cut through the park, then walk over to Columbus, and cab it downtown to the Baronet. Clutching the script like a machete, I soaked up the glorious autumn sunshine, admiring the trees with their leaves of burnished gold and deep russet, while envying the joggers and bikers, who were having fun this Saturday morning, and didn't have to deal with an over-the-hill prima donna who wanted to be ghostwritten into an ingenue.

If I didn't adjust my attitude, I just might have to kill her.

Five

"This show is sinking faster than the leading lady's last lift!" Larry Cotter, his lanky frame draped like unpressed pleats in his seventh row center seat, pointed to stage right, where Elaine Eden, dressed in a way too snug scarlet jumpsuit and matching helmet, paced, while yelling at an obviously nervous young woman who clutched what had to the largest cosmetic case in New York City. Even bigger than Gypsy Rose's.

Sitting next to Larry, yellow pad and red felt-tip pen in hand, I smiled, feeling pretty nervous myself.

"Of course the bitch blames my script," he said, "but then, the entire company does. Gareth is so disappointed with my material!"

"Larry, I read the script last night and—er—I loved most of it." I fell back into my lifelong habit of little ecru lies, but this one was whiter than most of them. I actually had liked several scenes. And God knows, he needed a vote of confidence. If providing Elaine Eden with more onstage sex would save his job—and mine—I'd tell more of my off-white lies to sell him on that, too.

Elaine's shouting jarred the dignity of the stately old

Baronet, a turn of the last century architectural gem that made many a modern theater-goer yearn to have lived in the Victorian era. However, at the moment, its plush red velvet seat provided small comfort.

Auturo Como and Dennis Kim huddled side by side, conferring, in the front row, and cast and crew members milled about the aisles, but no one attempted to silence the star's tirade.

"Isn't that Cynthia Malone up there with Elaine?" My stage whisper to Larry caused several heads to swivel in my direction.

Auturo jumped up and screamed, "Elaine, get over it! Where the hell is Philip Knight? What am I paying him those big bucks for, if not to baby-sit your tantrums? Why can't a producer ever find a goddamn director when he needs one!"

Larry sighed. "Yes, poor, dear Cynthia. In addition to all of her wardrobe duties, the makeup artist walked yesterday, and La Eden won't let anyone else near her surgery scars. Did you know, Jake, the woman has had three face-lifts and enough collagen injections to fill a crater? And, I have it on the best authority, last year half of Elaine's stomach and a third of her butt and thighs were trimmed down from heifer to calf size in Dr. Cut Away's private operating room."

That "cut away" remark was clever. The Fifth Avenue plastic surgeon du jour and, probably the one Elaine had used, was a Dr. Charles Caraway.

Afraid that Larry's voice had carried up to the stage, I stared at him, my emotions hovering between shock at what he said and awe that he'd said it.

But, sounding delighted with himself, he said, "Why, my dear, I understand she still has trouble sitting on a toilet seat!"

If Elaine heard either Larry or Auturo—and she would have to be stone deaf not to have heard the latter—she ignored both of them, and continued to act out her own drama. "Seams, Cynthia," she shouted, "you never let out the seams in this jumpsuit!"

"I did, Miss Eden, however, that was yesterday afternoon, before your late-night bourbon and bonbon binge!" Cynthia Malone's response upstaged the star and brought a burst of laughter from the audience.

Before Elaine could reply to that well-delivered line, Sebastian James, the internationally acclaimed award-winning actor, as well as bridegroom in three of Elaine Eden's weddings, stepped out of the wings, and staggered onto the stage. He wore a well-cut tuxedo, but his shoulders slumped and his belly bulged. Once-rugged features now looked like terrain that a herd had stampeded over. I wondered, was he in costume for his role as ambassador or hadn't he gone home last night?

"Even as a lass you were a bit bottom heavy, Elaine, and your girth has only increased, dramatically, with age. Furthermore, you're looking far too haggard to be believable as Suzy Q this morning, my dear. Is there time for a chin implant before opening night?" He slurred his words, and, though his charming Yorkshire accent sugarcoated his cruel comments, I realized that at 10:30 in the morning, Sir Sebastian was drunk as a skunk.

While I'd been too young to remember their first marriage, along with film and fight fans across the globe, I certainly remembered her fifth and his fourth wedding-go-round. A few years past their peak, the stars had remarried just in time to breathe new life into their stagnant careers.

The ceremony and reception had taken place in the castle that Elaine inherited from her third husband, a minor Spanish nobleman who claimed to have been descended from a love child of King Ferdinand's.

Every lesser level title and/or pretender to a European throne—real royalty sent regrets—had shown up at the masked ball that marked Elaine's marriage to the duke. He'd died during the honeymoon. Then, after less than a year of widowhood, she'd married her fourth husband, the Saudi billionaire's son, who'd spent their honeymoon dreaming that she was one of his sisters. Another short-term marriage.

But by her fifth and Sebastian's fourth marriage, Elaine had run out of clergymen willing to preside, so the honorable mayor of the tiny Spanish seaport town presided over their wedding ceremony at the castle. Photographs of Eden, James, and the beaming dignitary—savoring his fifteen minutes of fame—had graced the front page of every tabloid on three continents.

Within months, the battling Broadway stars were divorced again, each charging the other with adultery. Her new admirer was an Australian tennis star, twenty-five years her junior. His, a well-known feminist whom NOW immediately disavowed.

Neither married her/his lover, but instead remarried each other, early the following summer. Her sixth. His fifth. Their third. In Salt Lake City. A Mormon friend of the bride hosted a non-alcohol reception, as the groom—in what was far from his first attempt—had gone on the wagon. This time around, *The National Enquirer*'s caption under the picture of the overripe couple read: "At Long Last, a June Bride," says Elaine Eden.

That marriage ended in a drunken brawl—aboard a Greek shipping magnate's yacht, in the balmy waters off the Virgin Islands—involving a former secretary of state, a call girl, a case of French champagne, and a Havana cigar. Upon arrival, answering the purser's SOS, a US Coast Guard medic had to perform minor surgery. I've never read funnier punch lines than the *New York Post*'s reportage of that incident at sea. Even Mom had giggled.

But she hadn't laughed when telling me about Elaine and Sebastian's first marriage. They'd met while costarring in London in *Much Ado About Nothing*. Elaine had been Mrs. Brock Hunter, happily married to an early TV icon, and the mother of a six-year-old boy named Tristan. Sebastian, a British matinee idol, had married his grade-school sweetheart and was the father of a little girl.

Offstage, the costars' relationship turned out to be

much ado about lust. In short order, Brock Hunter—described by Elaine as "a nice boy, but not the man of my dreams"—and Cathy James—described by her about-to-be ex-husband as "a pretty, but simple, Yorkshire lass"—had been dragged into the messiest scandal since Liz and Eddie.

The first Mrs. James committed suicide a week after the divorce was final, and her parents disappeared with Sebastian and Cathy's daughter on the very day their former son-in-law married Elaine Eden.

Elaine's continued popularity with theater-goers, albeit often a love/hate relationship, seemed to prove that the American public had accepted adultery decades before a sitting president's indiscretion.

Now, watching Sebastian berate Elaine on stage, I almost felt pity for her.

Weaving, he stood between the two women. Cynthia Malone extended a hand as if to steady him, but he shoved it away, his bent elbow landing in Elaine's soft center. She stumbled, then spun around, somehow regaining control during that full circle, changing from an apparent victim back into a prima donna.

Just then Philip Knight, looking tall, tan, lean, and ready to referee, finally strode up the aisle. Elaine exerted her star power. "Where the hell have you been? I'm ready to rehearse my entrance."

I couldn't be the only one in the audience who immediately thought of Norma Desmond.

. . . . .

Amazingly, within five minutes, Philip Knight had directed Sebastian James back into the wings, asked the members of the orchestra to take their seats, and the dress rehearsal began.

I couldn't wait! Last night, while reading *Suzy Q*'s captivating opening scene, I hadn't dreamed that Elaine would perform the dangerous stunt that the script called for. Stealing bits from *Miss Saigon, Peter Pan,* and

Phantom of the Opera, our heroine, Suzy Q, would climb out of a chopper, scramble down a ladder, and arrive in the courtyard of the American embassy in Katmandu. I figured the leading lady would have her understudy do the dirty work, then, without the audience ever knowing the difference, the star would—somehow—switch places and take the credit. Sort of like my ghostwriting career.

But when the curtain opened, Elaine Eden, not an understudy, dangled halfway out of the helicopter that was suspended from unseen wires attached to the theater's very high ceiling. It hovered over a less-than-authentic backdrop of the Himalayas. The embassy and the courtyard, however, looked eerily beautiful, exactly as I had described them in *A Killing in Katmandu.*

Selby-Steed's earsplitting arrangement of trumpets, drums, and clashing cymbals accompanied the action. Where was Sir Gareth, anyway?

As the rest of the cast and crew applauded Elaine's entrance, Larry leaned over and whispered in my ear, "All through our earlier rehearsals, Elaine balked at doing this, said she was afraid of heights. I wonder how her boyfriend Philip talked her into it. Or maybe Auturo convinced her to make an *Entrance!* I must say, I'm flabbergasted to see her dangling there!"

"Me, too."

Elaine, facing a descent of more than forty feet, unfurled a thick rope ladder, dropping it down from the helicopter door. For a brief moment, her scarlet jumpsuit caught in a spotlight, we watched her swing back and forth, like a rider in the front seat on a Ferris wheel. I remembered the script called for a safe and graceful descent. But why a ladder made out of rope? What happened to high tech on Broadway? For God's sake, didn't Peter Pan fly around propelled by invisible wires? Was Auturo cutting corners?

Sebastian James, as the ambassador, stepped out of the embassy and into the courtyard to greet Suzy Q. Smiling. Waving up to her.

Our applause grew louder.

Elaine placed her right foot on the top rung of the ladder, gripping its sides. Suddenly, she was free-falling, landing hard, face first, at the feet of a stunned Sebastian James.

Still in a boozy haze, James stared at the crumpled heap of scarlet silk, while a surprisingly agile Philip Knight dashed up on stage. He knelt, taking Elaine Eden gently into his arms, as Cynthia Malone yelled from the front row, "Don't move her!"

Knight kissed Elaine's cheek, then bowed his head and cried, "My God! I think she's dead!"

Six

Sebastian threw up, some of his bile splattering Elaine's scarlet silk-clad legs. Then he retreated toward the embassy and plopped down on a wrought iron bench in the courtyard, facing away from the body, his sloped shoulders quivering.

Auturo, after barking orders at a 911 operator, threw his cell phone into the aisle, narrowly missing the head of a pretty young brunette dressed in the exact same jumpsuit that Elaine was wearing.

The woman, in turn, screamed, "Pig," then gave Auturo the finger, and kept on running toward the stage. Several of the crew chuckled, but their giggles quickly segued into an embarrassed silence.

Larry stood, but didn't move. "This changes everything! Think of all the rewriting we'll have to do now!"

Scrambling to get into the aisle, I stepped hard on Larry's foot as I pressed Ben's number and almost dropped my own cell phone.

Though I ran as fast as I could, while sending an SOS to Ben, Dennis had jumped into the orchestra pit, scaled the footlights, and arrived onstage before me.

From his bench on the sidelines, Sebastian groaned, "Cynthia, get me a drink!"

On cue, Cynthia entered from stage left, carrying a crystal glass filled with dark brown liquid. She must have poured it before he'd even asked. Her hand shook as she crossed the apron and circumnavigated, gingerly, behind the body.

The mysterious copycat in the scarlet jumpsuit and I trailed in Cynthia's wake.

A beat later, Gareth Selby-Steed entered from stage right. Ignoring Sebastian's shakes, Cynthia's soothing gestures, Philip's tears, Auturo's anger, the woman in red's scream, and Dennis's hand, held up in an attempt to halt him, he stepped over Elaine's body, almost knocking me down, and headed straight for the chopper.

Then, with his back to both his on- and offstage audience, Gareth bent and picked up something heavy. He stood, turned, and faced downstage, arms akimbo, straining to hold a section of the ladder in each hand. "Someone cut the top rung." He shook his head. Then laughed. "Now, who among us would have wanted to murder dear Elaine?"

The woman in red clapped, the sound echoing throughout the theater. "A role tailor-made for you, Sir Gareth. Perfect casting, you might say. But, I'm sure we all wonder, what will you do for an encore?"

"Everybody off the stage!" A big, burly uniformed cop yelled from the rear of the orchestra. "Move it!"

"The answer to my 911 call, I presume," Auturo Como said. For a man rumored to have mob connections, he sounded genuinely happy to see the police.

My cell phone rang. Obeying the cop's orders, I scurried into the wings.

"Are you okay?" Ben! My fickle heart fluttered, but romance wasn't on his mind. "What's happening there, Jake? I'm on my way to a crime scene."

Obviously not this one.

"Well, considering I just watched Elaine Eden fall from

a helicopter to her death, and it looks like she was murdered, I'm great, Ben. And how are you doing?"

"Where are you?"

"At the Baronet theater. Forty-sixth, between Broadway and Seventh. Elaine was rehearsing her entrance."

"Why are you there?"

"I'm helping rewrite the book for *Suzy Q.*"

"Have the uniforms arrived yet?" All business. Had he seen Dennis and me in the Waldorf lobby last night? Probably not. His partner seemed to have captured his total attention. And why should I care? But I did care. Way too much.

"As we speak."

"Good. I'm heading to my own crime scene. Broadway's not my beat, you know. The Nineteenth ends at Fifty-ninth Street."

"Yes, I know." So if the crime hadn't been committed in his precinct, it wasn't his concern. And, apparently, neither was I.

"I've got to go, Jake. Sorry about Elaine Eden. Give your mother my sympathy."

"Is that all you have to say?"

"I do have something else to say. Cooperate with the homicide detectives, Jake. Do not—I repeat—do not try to solve this murder. Murder and marriage don't mix."

A double meaning there? Seemingly talking about my mother and his father's upcoming wedding, but sending a message about any possible future marriage for him and me?

"Don't worry, Ben, I'm way too busy to play Nancy Drew! Tonight's the rehearsal, followed by Gypsy Rose's party for Mom and Aaron."

"Damn, I forgot. Now tell me again, why are we rehearsing on a Saturday night?"

"Father Newell is going away for a couple of days, and he really wanted to choreograph this himself—"

"Okay, I'll see you in church, kid." He hung up.

Staring out across the stage, now empty except for

Elaine's body, I watched Dennis, Auturo, and the police-man conferring in the theater's center aisle.

Wondering what I might have missed, I jammed my phone back into my tote bag, hurried out of the wings, and dashed down the stage left steps to join them.

During my dash, a homicide detective from Midtown North had arrived on the scene. Auturo the Angel clung to Dennis Kim like a man who believed he'd soon be needing a lawyer.

Detective Lieutenant John Mulroney had neither Ben Rubin's considerable charm nor his Antonio Banderas good looks. He nodded curtly when Dennis introduced us, "Take a seat, miss, I'll get to you later."

The deep frown lines etched across his forehead and around his mouth gave evidence of a man who seldom smiled. He held a cruller in one hand and a Starbucks cup in the other. Too cool to allow murder to interrupt his coffee break.

The burly cop had been drafted as Mulroney's secre-tary, and was jotting down Auturo's answers to the de-tective's questions. The producer, who'd seemed so glad to see the police arrive on the scene, now squirmed and stammered, having trouble spitting out his phone number.

From my front row vantage, I turned around to check out the rest of the crew, cast, and members of the or-chestra, who now sat, filling the first ten or twelve rows, waiting to be interviewed.

In the third row, Philip Knight wept silently and stared at the stage, his eyes locked on the body. Just then the medical examiner arrived, and someone—a cop or maybe a stagehand—closed the curtain. Philip continued to stare, as if he could see Elaine through the heavy velvet.

Behind Philip, Sebastian sipped from what looked like a fresh scotch. Cynthia sat next to him, stroking his arm and murmuring something in his ear.

Larry was still seventh row center with Sir Gareth next to him, ensconced in my former seat. The songwriter, us-ing what looked like a red Magic Marker, seemed to be editing the script. Had Larry been serious about our re-writing *Suzy Q*?

The lady in red sat alone in the rear. Who the hell was she? Elaine's understudy? Now wouldn't that be an *All About Eve* motive!

Everyone looked guilty and acted antsy. Including me.

But in less time then *Suzy Q*'s three-act rehearsal would have taken, we'd all given our statements and been dispatched with the same reservation from Lt. Mulroney: "Expect a visit from Homicide today or tomorrow."

Seven

Barrymore's, on the north side of Forty-fifth Street, right off Eighth Avenue, has been part of the Times Square scene for as long as I can remember. After seeing my first-ever Broadway musical, I'd ordered my first-ever cheeseburger there, over twenty-five years ago.

Popular with performers and their audiences alike, the pub has remained a favorite pre- or post-theater stop for Mom, Gypsy Rose, and me.

One night, when I was a teenager, the three of us had dropped by for a post-theater supper and found ourselves seated next to the late Jason Robards. My celebrity crazy mother asked him to autograph her playbill and he wound up joining us for coffee. Barrymore's was that kind of place.

So when Dennis suggested that we stop there for a burger and a beer, I agreed, knowing the pub's good food and friendly atmosphere would make me feel better fast.

We sat up front in one of the wooden booths directly across from the bar. Not so jammed as it would be later tonight, but still not a stool available. Several customers were eating at the bar. Others were watching a football game. In the background, muted but marvelous, Jimmy Durante sang "As Time Goes By," from the *When Harry Met Sally* soundtrack.

Dennis grinned at me. "Can't escape that song, can we?"

I had no time for romance. Starving, I glanced at my watch. "Almost three-thirty, no wonder I'm so damn hungry."

"You're always hungry, Jake," Dennis laughed, "and I think murder fuels your appetite."

"Could be," I said, turning to the waitress, whose platinum hairstyle reminded me of Elaine's. "I'd like an order of onion rings with my cheeseburger."

"Instead of the french fries?" The waitress laughed, too. I knew her by sight, if not by name; she usually worked the night shift.

"Hell, no. In addition to."

When our drinks were served, I asked Dennis, "Okay, whodunit? And why? Looked like most of *Suzy Q*'s cast and crew might have motives. Elaine Eden, certainly, never won any awards for Miss Congeniality. No one in that theater, except for her fiancé, Philip Knight, shed a tear."

Dennis sipped his beer, then smirked. "Yet he might have had the best motive of all . . ."

"What? Tell me, Dennis, or you'll never live to sing 'As Time Goes By' again!"

"Auturo and Gareth tell me that Philip Knight, always a notorious swordsman, has not pulled in his reins during his golden years. The old boy has been cheating on his bride-to-be."

And I'd totally bought into the director's crocodile tears. "But Knight seemed so distraught . . ."

"Being distraught doesn't necessarily mean someone has always been faithful, does it, Jake? If I died, wouldn't you cry?"

Feeling frustrated and outsmarted, I said, "And Philip Knight was fooling around with . . . ?"

Dennis looked smug. "The lady in red."

"Who the hell is she?"

"Morgan Drake, a very talented, very beautiful young actress."

Unbridled, not to mention completely irrational, jealously hit my toes with a visible jolt.

"What's wrong, Jake?"

"Nothing. . . . A cramp or something." I rubbed my toes. "It's nothing. . . . Gone now." I took a long swallow of beer. "Is this Morgan Drake Elaine Eden's understudy?"

"No, she's playing the ingenue role . . . well, I guess a little older than an ingenue—you know, the Kit Marlowe role. Gareth says Morgan steals the show every time she steps on stage."

"If she's not Elaine's understudy, then why was she running around in that red jumpsuit?"

"Good question. Let's hope Lt. Mulroney asks her that. Though I don't think he's as bright as Ben is, do you?"

Only the arrival of my cheeseburger, fries, and onion rings spared Dennis Kim from a biting retort.

As the waitress plopped a plate down in front of me, filled with enough food to feed five, she said, "I know you, don't I? My name's Meg. You usually come in with your mother and that fortune-teller lady, Gypsy Rose Liebowitz, right?"

I hoped Gypsy Rose wasn't having a psychic moment. She so resented being referred to as a fortune-teller. I smiled and nodded.

"Yeah," Meg said. "Don't you just love her bookstore up there in Carnegie Hill? I like, you know, hardly ever leave my zip code, but your friend has the best collection of spiritual books in the entire city."

Who knew our waitress had a spiritual side?

"Yes, Gypsy Rose stocks the best writers in their fields, doesn't she?" I speared an onion ring.

"*The Road Less Traveled* is the greatest book ever! Changed my life. I take responsibility for my own actions now. Realizing I'm part of the worldwide spiritual community. That I have a destiny, you know?"

Chewing, I nodded again, wishing that Dennis would take a little responsibility here and answer Meg.

Silence.

But Meg wasn't finished sharing with us. "Hey, don't think I'm a busybody or an eavesdropper or anything, but when I was passing by before, I overheard you two talking about that bitch Elaine Eden. Is she dead? After what happened here last night, I wouldn't be surprised if someone bumped her off." She giggled nervously. "Actually, lots of people wanted that woman dead. Starting with our wait staff."

I swallowed fast. "Meg, I'm Jake O'Hara, this is Dennis Kim, an attorney." At her frown, I added, "But he's on the right side in this case. And he's a good guy. I've known him forever, since we were kids. Please believe me, Gypsy Rose would want you to do the right thing. You need to tell us what happened here last night."

"Well . . ."

"This could be the most spiritual thing you'll ever do, while still on this plane." Dennis shook his head, but I ignored him. "Meg, don't miss this chance to make a difference! Your moment to shine this time around, before your soul travels to the world beyond . . ."

"Okay," she said, "I have one more station to serve, then I'll tell the chef I'm taking a break. I'll be back in five minutes."

I wolfed down the cheeseburger in four. Between bites, I tried to convert Dennis to my point of view. When I finished eating, he handed me a Pepcid AC.

Meg slid into the booth next to me and ordered a ginger ale, explaining that she never drank on duty. "Okay, before I say anything, you tell me, did someone kill Elaine Eden?"

"I don't know. Maybe. This morning, in the theater, she had an accident, fell from a helicopter that was dangling from the rafters, and landed on stage, headfirst. Yes, she's dead. And, yes, it looks suspicious." As I spoke, it occurred to me that Elaine Eden might have committed suicide. I immediately rejected that idea. The lady didn't strike me as suicidal.

"God! Well, the cast from *Suzy Q* hangs out here, you know." Meg frowned. "Shouldn't I be telling this to the police?"

"Yes!" Dennis said, placing his beer glass down on the table with what I considered unnecessary and excessive emphasis. "Call Detective Mulroney at the Midtown North Precinct and tell him everything you know."

"Dennis is right, Meg. Make that phone call just as soon as we leave—but since Elaine was an old acquaintance of my mother's, and I'm working on *Suzy Q*, trying to save the show, I do have a vested interest here . . ."

Sounded flimsy at best, but I'd sensed Meg wanted to spill it all now, and I was right.

She lit a Pall Mall, then said, "Unsavory bunch, aren't they?"

I nodded. "They sure are."

Dennis drained my beer.

"Sebastian James, that old windbag has-been, was here last night verbally abusing his ex-wife." Meg grimaced. "His favorite sport."

"What time would that have been?" Probably right after Elaine had left Mom's lesser literary lights salon.

"Late. About ten or so. Elaine had just joined Philip Knight at the booth in front of this one. He'd been waiting for her for almost an hour. But that aging ingenue Morgan Drake had been entertaining him. A very cozy couple. Knight had been directing Drake's hand movements under the table, but she made a fast exit when Elaine stormed in, all bent out of shape."

"Do you know why Elaine was upset?"

"No." Meg inhaled deeply. "That bitch always had a burr up her butt. Last night was no different."

I wondered.

"Anyway, no sooner was Elaine seated than Sebastian

left his table, stumbled over to hers, and said, 'The American theater's finest moment will be your funeral.' Then, for his finale, he fell headfirst into Philip Knight's mashed potatoes.''

"Damn!" I knocked over my water glass. "That sounds like a death threat, doesn't it?"

Dennis dropped his look of disdain, and jumped in. "Was Sebastian James alone?"

"No." Meg dropped her cigarette into Dennis's empty beer bottle. "That Cynthia, the wardrobe mistress . . . I doubt she's his real mistress, but, even though she's so much younger, they do have this weird nursemaid/child kind of thing going on there. Anyway, as usual, she'd kept Sebastian company last night. After his scene, she pulled his face up from the bowl of potatoes, cleaned him off, and got him the hell out of here."

I asked, "And what about Elaine Eden? What did she do? How did she react?"

"Like the grande dame pain in the butt that she was. Eden just paraded straight over to Liz Smith's table and, cool as a cucumber, asked her to not include 'that tawdry incident' in her column."

Eight

Going from Elaine Eden's dress rehearsal that had ended in her death to Mom's wedding rehearsal that would end with a gala dinner at Gypsy Rose's town house called for a role reversal.

I showered, washed and conditioned my hair, then let Mom—wearing hot rollers, a green facial mask, white bunny slippers, and a plaid housecoat that had to be circa 1958—blow it dry and apply my makeup. All too soon, she'd be spending most of her time in DC. I realized how much I would miss her fussing and even her nagging.

As she waved a blush brush, she shared her personal powder philosophy with me, for at least the hundredth, but I hoped not the last, time. "Always invest in the very best brushes, Jake. A wide, wonderful, soft one that will make a smooth, clean sweep across your cheek. Think of it as a magic wand that transforms a drab skin tone into a glowing complexion. Suck in your lower face, darling. I want to create the illusion of cheekbones."

Aaron had called Mom with the news of Elaine's unexpected demise, but I thought she seemed more curious than concerned.

"Ben told Aaron that Elaine had fallen from a helicopter. So *Miss Saigon*! Did Sir Gareth Selby-Steed lift the score from that, too? Were you an eyewitness, Jake? Death does seem to rain on the O'Hara women's parade, doesn't it? Especially violent death."

I couldn't take issue with that.

By the time Mom had completed my toilette, she knew what I knew. And wanted in on the action. Her Miss Marple aiding and abetting my Nancy Drew.

"*Cherchez la femme,* Jake. Some ex-wife, jilted lover, or former girlfriend of one of the many men that Elaine Eden has seduced, then stolen. They must be legion."

"Whoever killed her had to have been on the scene today, Mom."

"Why would those two things be mutually exclusive? One of those brokenhearted, discarded women could have been at the rehearsal. What if she were now a member of the *Suzy Q* cast or crew?"

I've always suspected that Miss Marple was much smarter than Nancy Drew!

The intercom interrupted us. I left Mom to shed the bunny slippers, rollers, and green guck, and finish dressing. Still in my robe, I dashed across the living room and into the foyer to answer it. The bridegroom and the best man were waiting in the lobby. Feeling really nervous about facing Ben, I buzzed them up.

Then, putting murder on hold, I ran back into my room to check out Mom's "cosmetic artwork" before I opened the door.

I've always loved men in navy blue blazers and gray flannel pants. Dressing down according to Ralph Lauren. Aaron, something of a clotheshorse, had added a wine-and-gray silk tie. The gray in the print matched his hair. Exactly. By design, rather than accident, would be my bet.

His son was no slouch, either. His well-cut suit as black as his hair. From the first time I'd laid eyes on Ben Rubin, his strikingly Latino look had reminded me of Antonio Banderas. Never as much as tonight. Ben had inherited

those great genes from his mother. She'd died a few years
ago.

In the late 1930s, when she'd been a toddler, her family, fleeing Franco, left Spain and arrived in America. I
wondered if she'd had Ben's sexy laugh, too. Though he
seldom spoke of her, he always kept her picture in his
wallet. Oval face, big doe eyes, dark hair, parted in the
middle and piled high under a lace mantilla.

"You two look very dashing!" I planted chaste kisses
on each of their cheeks. "Why don't you grab a seat while
I hustle Mom along?"

"I'm in the bathroom, Jake," my mother sang out, "but
I'm almost ready. Be out in a second."

Right.

How does she keep her bedroom so damn neat? Not so
much as an errant piece of paper.

Sweeping around the room, my eyes landed on the
dresser and locked on to my father's smiling face. He and
Mom had posed in a Buick convertible, circa 1959. Her
long blonde hair windblown. His arm draped over her
shoulder, one hand on the wheel. The black-and-white
photograph could have been a movie still. They looked
so glamorous, so young, and so in love.

I sighed, wondering if maybe Ben's mother and my
father had run into each other up there in the world beyond.

Maybe Gypsy Rose could ask them.

Tears fell. I wiped them away with my fingertips, then
stared into the mirror at the streaks of black mascara running down my face, ruining my carefully crafted cheekbones.

Now I'd have to repair the damage and hope that Mom
wouldn't notice.

. . . . .

The scent from red roses, arranged in tall vases that
had decorated the altar during the just ended Saturday
evening Mass, permeated the aisles. Bathed in the glow

of candlelight, the small church looked beautiful. So did the bride-to-be. She seemed to not walk, but float, in perfect step to the organ music. Mr. Kim, absolutely beaming, escorted Mom down the aisle. Where the hell was Dennis? As an usher, he should be here, too.

Gypsy Rose and I had led the way, and now stood on the bride's side of the altar, while Aaron and Ben stood on the groom's, with Father Newell in the middle. All awaiting Mom's arrival.

Mrs. McMahon, our nosy neighbor who never missed a wake or a wedding—whether she'd been invited or not—sat in the front row, scribbling in a notebook. Her mustard yellow hat, the shape of a flying saucer, seemed to defy gravity.

"Isn't it breaking tradition for the bride-to-be to actually come down the aisle during the wedding rehearsal?" Gypsy Rose whispered in my ear. However, her whisper echoed around the church.

Mrs. McMahon stood and, as if giving testimony, said, "That's right! You should have a stand-in, Maura. Both bad form and bad luck to do it yourself, you know!"

Father Newell frowned at her. She sat down, just as Mom and Mr. Kim reached her pew.

"Isn't there some viewing in Queens or Brooklyn that you're missing tonight, Mrs. McMahon?" Mr. Kim sounded icy. Almost mean. So out of character for the sweet poet/greengrocer. "Mourning becomes you, but this is a happy occasion."

You can't insult Mrs. M. "Just trying to help out here," she said, then jotted something in her red notebook.

Stationed as sentinel in our lobby or at her kitchen window, she fancied herself to be the conscience of our co-op and, maybe, all of Carnegie Hill. For the last ten years, most of our conversations have consisted of Mrs. M's attempts to lure me away from my career as a ghostwriter—"No name, no fame, no gain, Jake"—and to entice me into a career with Mary Kay, where her oldest daughter's cosmetic sales have earned the company's biggest bonus . . . a pink Cadillac.

My mother has always tolerated the busybody better than I ever could.

Father Newell had a real flair for drama, and loved hearing his own voice. He almost had Mom and Aaron married, when he caught himself mid-sentence. "Can't get carried away, this is only the rehearsal!"

An hour after we began—the actual wedding ceremony wouldn't run that long—we left the church and headed up to Gypsy Rose's town house for the rehearsal dinner.

Still no Dennis. I shrugged. He'd just have to wing his role.

Nine

Gypsy Rose's turn of the last century redbrick town house on the northeast corner of Ninety-third Street and Madison Avenue has been my second home since I was eight years old. With the money that the late Louie Liebowitz had left her, she'd opened her New Age bookstore/tearoom—better scones than at the Plaza's Palm Court—on the first floor, and created a magnificent residence on the three upstairs levels. Mostly from the bookstore's profits.

We were in her second-floor kitchen, which ran the length of the house from south to north and the depth from east to west. Though the open space flowed graciously and seemingly endlessly from one section into the next, each area served its own distinct purpose and possessed its own unique charm.

Tonight's dinner party was in Gypsy Rose's huge dining area. The guest list reflected Mom's favorite people.

Three round tables of four were covered in floor-length ivory damask cloths, and set with cream-color Wedgwood china and Waterford crystal glasses. In each of her centerpieces—small Tiffany crystal heart bowls—she'd floated a single perfect white gardenia.

A piano player had been briefed on Mom's preferred composers. Cole, Noel, and Rodgers and Hart. Flames danced in the huge brick fireplace, though, on this cool, but not cold, October night, I had a hunch that Gypsy Rose had turned the air conditioner on as well.

I checked out the engraved place cards as a waiter passed around cocktails and canapés. Our hostess, ever the diplomat, had not put Ben and Dennis near each other. I would be sitting with Mom, Aaron, and Ben. Gypsy Rose, her current ardent, albeit unrequited, admirer, Christian Holmes, devout atheist and religion editor at *Manhattan Magazine*, Mr. Kim, and Too Tall Tom, a how-to ghost and one of the city's best paid carpenters, as well as my best friend, would be at the middle table.

Gypsy Rose came up behind me, slipping an arm around my waist. "My mama didn't raise any dopey daughters, Jake. As the hostess, I get to sit with three guys."

I moved on to the third table. "You stuck Dennis between Modesty and Jane!"

"Well, hell, if the ghosts drive him crazy, I figured he can talk shop with Rickie Romero, right?"

My deep guffaw received a dirty look from Mom. "Gypsy Rose, do you think a paroled former cat burglar and a practicing entertainment attorney have a lot in common?"

"Don't you?" She hustled off to check on the lamb roasting in the kitchen area's open hearth.

My cell phone rang. Speak of the devil.

"Sorry. I tried to call, but I guess you all had your phones turned off in church. They towed my car!" Dennis sounded aggrieved.

"Where are you?"

"Way the hell over on the West Side. At first I'd thought it was stolen, but then I grabbed a cab, and headed over here to the pound."

"And?"

"And they can't find it. No record that any Rolls-Royce ever arrived. Jesus, maybe someone did swipe it! Anyway, this neighborhood is tough. I've been walking and walking. Can't find a cab, but I knew you'd be worried—"

"Frantic!" The laughter I'd been trying to suppress escaped. Loud and raucous.

"Is this funny, Jake?"

"We were thinking of hiring an understudy. Ushering is a tough part to play, you know."

He hung up.

"Hello, Jake!" Modesty arrived, dressed in one of her more attractive shroudlike numbers, black silk, actually, and eerily becoming. She carried a platter of homemade brownies. Rickie Romero, wearing his own basic black "uniform" and the look of love, trailed behind her, toting two gallons of Edy's French vanilla.

Though many members of our Ghostwriters Anonymous group considered Modesty miserable—true enough, though she has adjusted her attitude somewhat since Rickie moved in with her—and a misogynist—you could make a case there, too—I liked her. Over the last year, she has become one of my best friends. For some reason, I'm one of the few women she can tolerate. Maybe because I keep involving her in murder. And I planned to again.

"Hey, Modesty," I said. "Your hair looks great."

I hadn't seen her in some time. Dennis and I had gone to Venice, then Mom, Gypsy Rose, and I had spent a month in the Hamptons. A last hurrah "girly" vacation. When we returned, Rickie had whisked Modesty off on a tour of Druid ruins in Ireland, and Transylvanian castles, visiting Modesty's ancestral roots. Travel/genealogy one-upmanship.

Her short pale red crop of curls had grown. Chin length and kind of wild, framing her light green eyes in a soft halo. I peered closer. "My God, Modesty, are you wearing makeup?"

Under the lightly applied rouge, I could see her blush.

"Hmm." She stared at her feet. New sandals. With heels yet! What the hell . . .

Rickie placed a protective arm around her shoulder. "I gave Modesty an Elizabeth Arden facial and a makeover for our sixth-month anniversary. Guess what we're doing to celebrate our seventh?"

They'd met on St. Patrick's Day, so that would be next week. October 17.

"We're getting married!" Last June, Rickie had said they would marry, but I guess I hadn't wanted to believe it.

"Some guys have all the luck!" Dennis Kim came up behind me, managing to kiss the back of my neck while shaking the prospective groom's hand.

Modesty said, "And, of course, you'll be my maid of honor."

"Always the bridesmaid, Jake?" Ben Rubin had joined our merry little band.

"Excuse me," I said, backing away from all of them. "I'm not feeling very well." Then I dashed to the nearest of Gypsy Rose's four bathrooms, sat on the john, and sobbed.

Well, I started to, but Modesty, rapping on the door, interrupted me. "Let me in, Jake!"

If I didn't, my mother might be next, so I opened the door.

"What the hell is wrong with you?" Her creased forehead belied her sharp tones.

"I wish I knew."

Modesty almost giggled, so out of character for her. "I'll bet Dennis Kim and Ben Rubin wished you knew, too."

"Is that my problem?"

"Listen, I'm no expert, but even a romantic misfit like me, new to the nuances of love, and engaged to a former cat burglar, can see that being in love with two guys, while your mother's about to marry one of their fathers, might be considered a problem." She handed me a tissue. "Of course, I don't think either of them is worthy enough to be the object of your affection."

Her concern both surprised and touched me.

"Thanks," I said, and blew my nose.

Modesty sat on a small velvet stool, and kept on talking. "You have to put your problems on the shelf until after your mother's wedding. Yoga will help. Then we'll check out your charkas. And we'll figure out what happened to Elaine. That will cheer you up. But you have to forget about love, until after Maura says 'I do.' "

I smiled. "And we'll go shopping for my dress for your wedding!" She actually let me hug her.

. . . . .

I finished the last of Gypsy Rose's roast lamb and saffron rice. A messy love life hadn't affected my appetite. Nor Ben's. And no lack of lighthearted chatter. Our main topic of conversation during dinner had been the wedding.

Ben's champagne toast, a touching tribute to Mom and Aaron's devotion to family, friends, and each other, had brought tears to everyone's eyes but mine. Modesty was so right. No more tears for me.

I promised myself that I wouldn't even think about my feelings for either Ben or Dennis until after the wedding reception. But I suspected that might be a promise meant to be broken. Still, Modesty's offer to help investigate Elaine Eden's death had perked me up. Nothing like delving into murder to take my mind off men.

"You're very quiet, Jake," my mother said. "Too quiet!"

The piano player segued from "It Had to Be You" to "As Time Goes By." Ben smiled. "A little more champagne, Jake? Or would my future stepsister like to dance? Your favorite song, isn't it?"

"Good," Aaron said. "Maura and I will join you!"

As Ben drew me into his arms, a faint scent of Ivory

soap aroused warm memories. A heart full of passion, jealousy, and hate told a head full of good intentions to take a hike.

Fortunately, Too Tall Tom cut in.

At five four, I only came up to his chest, but his style and grace, not to mention excellent fox-trotting technique, made us look good.

As we dipped, he said, "Modesty tells me you need a diversion." Too Tall Tom glanced over at Ben, who now sat alone at the table, sipping champagne. "I'm here to provide one."

"One what?"

"Diversion. A big-time diversion." He spun me around. "Tristan Hunter. Elaine Eden and Brock Hunter's son."

I almost tripped coming back to him, but he whirled me in the other direction, turning an awkward moment into a graceful save. "Really! Do you know him?"

"I did. Biblically, as well as socially."

This time I did trip. "Where? When? What . . . ?"

Too Tall Tom led me to a quiet sitting area, overstuffed sofas, rattan tables, good reading lamps. Empty now. We sank into one of the sofas.

The only passion I had to contend with at the moment was an insatiable curiosity. "So?"

"In Chelsea. Over fifteen years ago, long before Chelsea became chic. We were nineteen and students at the School of Visual Arts and, as it turned out, we were both living at the Leo House."

"The Leo House? That used to be a hotel for priests traveling to New York, right? I think it's still run by nuns."

He nodded.

"Wasn't that rather spartan for Elaine's son?"

"Jake, he ended up in a monastery in Tibet, didn't he? Tristan always preferred to keep it simple. A hell of a good kid, rebelling against his mother's lifestyle. The year she remarried Sebastian James, Tristan quit school and entered the temple."

"But you stayed in touch? Why haven't you ever mentioned him?"

"No, we didn't stay in touch. Too painful. He'd been very important to me and he took off without saying good-bye!"

"So you haven't seen him in fifteen years?"

"That's what I'm trying to tell you, Jake. I saw him this morning! About two hours before his mother's murder!"

Ten

By 12:30 A.M., Mom had gone to bed and Rickie had gone to his consultant job, inspecting Tiffany's late-night security system. God knows, they'd hired the expert in his field.

The ghosts and I were in my living room, sipping herbal tea and dissecting Elaine Eden's death.

"If this was murder," Too Tall Tom said, "and that woman was far too shallow to commit suicide, Tristan Hunter had many, many motives for killing off his mom, including money! But I know he didn't do this!"

"When it looks like a duck," Jane said, "and it walks like a duck . . ."

Too Tall Tom paced and pointed a long finger at Jane. "Tristan is no killer! He's the sweetest, most gentle soul that God ever made—"

Even while interrupting, I weighed my words. "Fifteen years is a long time. People change."

"Not Tristan!" Too Tall Tom continued pacing. From the foot of the steps that led into the living room to the archway into the dining room, where he made a military pivot and repeated the routine. "He hasn't changed at all.

Exudes goodness. And he's way too naive to help himself! We have to find out who cut that bloody rope!"

Modesty patted the empty space next to her on the sofa and said, "For God's sake, sit down."

To my surprise, Too Tall Tom obeyed her order. "Okay," Modesty continued, "now, tell us exactly what you and your former lover talked about this morning. And why exuding goodness—what a vile thought—would preclude someone from being a killer."

"I haven't got time to be dragged into another murder," Jane said. "I'm on deadline."

"Your deadline be damned!" Modesty waved her hand, dismissing Jane's objection as if swatting a fly. "You've been shopping at Bloomingdale's and Bergdorf every single day this week, haven't you?"

Jane said, "Well, only in better dresses. I haven't been able to find the right dress for Maura's wedding . . . and now, despite the fact that my book is due November first, I have to buy yet another outfit for your wedding."

Jane had my empathy. Though she could be a real pain in the butt, driving us all crazy, sneaking off to shop. When Jane had started collecting great royalties from ghosting a series of very successful self-help books, she'd morphed from a little brown wren into a fashion flamingo. Tonight she wore a wonderful gray wool Ellen Tracy suit, with a Fendi pouch bag and Charles Jordan pumps. A composite of international design.

Sounding as if he seriously resented being wrested from the center of attention by Jane and Modesty's squabbling, Too Tall Tom said, "Tristan told me he'd returned home to make peace with his mother."

I asked, "Did he say how he planned to do that?"

"Yes. He was on his way to the theater, to invite his mother to dinner at the Four Seasons. Tristan wanted to reach out to her. Forgive her. Ask her to forgive him."

Modesty said, "I wonder if they had their little chat before she fell. Anyway, with her being dead and all . . .

I guess he had to make other plans for dinner. Speaking of plans, did you and Tristan have any?"

"Yes. For brunch at Tavern on the Green tomorrow." Too Tall Tom glanced at his watch. "Actually, today."

I said, "I think you should keep that date. And keep an open mind. If Tristan's not our guy, he may know—or suspect—who is."

"You guys have made me feel really guilty and, probably, have violated about six of our Ghostwriter Anonymous steps!" Jane smoothed her skirt. "However, I can see how Jake's two maid of honor assignments while ghosting a script might make my schedule appear light . . . so, how can I help? But make it snappy. I have an appointment at Saks at ten tomorrow morning."

I didn't bother to tell her that Elaine's death—no doubt—had ended my ghostwriting assignment. "Thanks, Jane. Okay, as I see it, here's the cast of suspects, beginning with the most likely."

Modesty opened her bag and pulled out a pad and pen. I felt a surge of excitement.

"Elaine's thrice ex-husband, Sebastian James, has been auditioning for the role of her killer for years. They hated each other for decades, especially between their marriages. Since the last divorce, their rage has gone totally over the top. He was verbally abusive—cruel, in fact—both this morning in front of a large audience and Friday night in front of the waitress at Barrymore's, Philip Knight, Cynthia Malone—the show's wardrobe mistress—and even, for God's sake, Liz Smith."

Too Tall Tom frowned. "What about *Suzy Q*'s director? Wasn't Knight Eden's current squeeze? The thought of bedding that old bag ought to be enough to drive a straight guy to murder!"

I laughed. "Not a nice man. All gushy over Elaine today, and acted crushed by her demise, but according to Meg, that's the Barrymore's waitress, he'd been crawling like a bug all over Morgan Drake before his fiancée arrived at the restaurant last night."

Jane asked, "Who's Morgan Drake?"

"Kind of an overripe ingenue. Plays the second female lead. Sexy as hell. Weird. She showed up today in an exact duplicate of Elaine's red jumpsuit. The one she died in . . ."

Modesty said, "Is this Morgan Drake also Elaine's understudy?"

"No." I shook my head. "Actually, I haven't even met the understudy yet." I finished my now tepid tea. "But I wondered why she wasn't there this morning. Larry told me Elaine had never done that opening stunt."

"Aha!" Too Tall Tom grinned. "Maybe the understudy murdered Elaine. The Eve Harrington angle. So in keeping with the theatrical setting."

Jane stood and stretched. "I hope we're almost done. But who's Larry?"

"The man whose job I took."

"Then it would be you he'd want dead, not Elaine," Jane laughed. "Look, I'm out of here."

"I only have a couple more to go." Knowing Jane did freelance profiles for "news" magazines, I rushed on. "You might find a hot suspect . . . and a hot celebrity interview."

She sat back down. "Whom did you have in mind?"

"For starters, Auturo Como, the angel from hell. He'd lost millions investing in Elaine Eden. Or Sir Gareth Selby-Steed. According to him, Elaine had mucked up his music. Your angle could be how he fired his lover."

Usually, a ghostwriter never breaks her confidentiality agreement—indeed, in most cases, she'd be sued—but I knew my *Suzy Q* script doctor contract would hit the gossip columns by tomorrow morning. Poor Larry.

Jane purred but said nothing.

"Think how colorful your profile—"

"Jake!" Too Tall Tom's six feet eight inches suddenly stood imposingly above me. "I want to question Selby-Steed!"

Damn. Here we go again, fighting over who gets which

suspect. . . . Now, how the hell can I smooth this . . .

Modesty leaped up, her tiny figure considerably less imposing than Too Tall Tom's. "Cynthia Malone. *Suzy Q*'s wardrobe woman. I knew I'd heard that name before And I've just remembered where we met."

"Where?" Too Tall Tom, diverted for the moment, asked.

"At the Gothic Romance Writers Weekend in Wycoff."

"As in New Jersey?" Jane gave a slight shudder.

Modesty crossed in front of me and got right into Jane's face. "A how-to ghost shouldn't be such a goddamn snob! It's a wonderful conference. Why, over that weekend I whittled my Gothic mystery manuscript down to eleven hundred pages."

Since her page count had been well over 2000, this was no small accomplishment.

As Jane drew back in mock horror, I said, "So, Modesty, what did you think about Cynthia Malone? Did you talk to her? Why had she attended that conference? Is she a writer as well as a wardrobe mistress?"

Turning her back to Jane, Modesty said, "Malone sat next to me in the Bodice Ripping Workshop. She wore a Barbara Cartland hat. Circa the sixties. At first I thought she was British."

"Funny, so did I."

"She had some talent. Wrote good sex." Coming from Modesty, high praise. "But always about a younger woman/older man relationship. And she behaved the same way in real life."

Jane, sounding really interested, said, "Give us an example."

Modesty repositioned herself so Jane could see her, too. I smiled, aware that I'd just witnessed a truce.

"Cynthia Malone had this obscene thing for older men," Modesty said. "Positively fawned over the old boy who led the conference. Fetching his coffee, running his errands, straightening up his papers. Messy old coot."

"Strange," I said. "She treated Sebastian James the same way. Doted on him . . ."

"Gets on your nerves real quick, doesn't it?" Modesty shook her red head. "On first impression, I thought Malone might be okay, but by the end of the weekend, I hated her."

As if any of us would have expected Modesty-the-misogynist to feel any other way about her Gothic romance competitor.

"I'm shocked. Shocked," Too Tall Tom said.

We all laughed. Even Modesty.

Ten minutes later, the ghosts, each with a short list of murder suspects, went home. And I went to bed to mull over mine, once again counting suspects instead of sheep.

Eleven

The phone woke me up. I rolled over to glance at the alarm clock on the rattan table next to my bed. Mom had called the room British Colonial when she redecorated—using part of a hefty advance I'd received last fall—replacing my perfectly fine maple furniture. My new bed was swathed in some kind of gauzy white mosquito netting and my mahogany/rattan dresser and armoire, according to Mom, "combined Victorian elegance with Caribbean charm."

Nine-thirty. Good. I'd slept late. The last time I'd checked the clock, it had been 3:00 A.M.

I picked up the phone on the fourth ring.

"I didn't wake you, did I?" Dennis asked, without so much as a hint of apology if he had.

"Yes, you did."

"The pound called. The Rolls is there. I guess the cops went joyriding before bringing it in. I'm on my way to pick it up."

"You didn't wake me up to tell me that!"

"Well . . ."

"Dennis!"

"The show's going on, Jake, opening as scheduled on Thursday night. You still have a job."

"I do not. My rewrites were for Elaine—"

"Your contract is with Auturo Como and Sir Gareth Selby-Steed. Not with the deceased."

"No. No. No!"

"Since the Baronet is now officially a crime scene, Auturo had to rent an empty theater to rehearse in. The Globe. Over between Ninth and Tenth. On Forty-fifth Street."

"And where did he find the money to do that? Isn't he broke? I thought *Suzy Q* had run out of cash."

"Get this. Auturo and Gareth had taken out an act of God insurance policy on Elaine Eden. To protect their investment. They'll collect big time on her unexpected demise. And Auturo has just finished telling me that murder makes for bigger box office."

"Isn't he afraid Detective Mulroney might consider that insurance policy to be a motive?"

"He sure as hell didn't sound nervous. If he's afraid, he's a better actor than Sebastian."

I sat up. "Maybe he is."

"Of course, Jake, you realize that the show will need a bit more rewriting. Skewing younger."

Curiosity was my curse. I propped up the pillows. "So the understudy's going on in place of Elaine? A star is born?"

"Knowing how much you love a mystery, here's one: A star is born, but it's not Peggy Malfa."

"That's the understudy's name?"

"Yes . . . but it won't be up in lights."

"Morgan Drake!" I moved to the edge of the bed.

"Score one for Nancy Drew. And that was Philip Knight's casting call. He insisted that Morgan Drake play Suzy Q or he'd walk. Como and Selby-Steed didn't want to hire a new director this late in the game. Nor did they want to close the show—both have way too much money invested in it—so they agreed. Especially interesting, since

Philip had been playing patty-cake with Morgan the very night before his fiancée took that tumble!"

I brushed my bangs out of my eyes. "When do they begin rehearsals?"

"At eleven A.M."

"Today?"

"Rise and shine, sleepyhead. I'll pick you up in an hour."

. . . . .

A lingering scent of burned bagels filled the kitchen. I made a cup of tea and toasted—to perfection, if I did say so, myself—a cinnamon raisin bagel.

Mom had left me a note, saying she'd gone to ten o'clock Mass and reminding me that we had another party tonight. At seven. Dennis would host this one. Cocktails and dinner at the River Café. I'd totally forgotten about that. And Dennis hadn't mentioned it, either. I wondered if he'd remembered. Mom's note—actually, more of a newsletter—went on to tell me that after church she and Aaron would be going to the Central Park Zoo, where they'd feed the seals at noon. She'd packed a human lunch, too.

I sighed. When I'd been a kid, Mom and I used to spend almost every fall Sunday in the park.

I pulled on jeans and a black turtleneck, then decided a sweater would be too warm and changed to a long-sleeved tan cotton shirt, topped with a matching lightweight wool blazer.

Dennis, most certainly double-parked, buzzed up at ten-thirty. Damn, the button had fallen off my jeans. I shouted through the intercom, "I'll be down in a minute," and ran into Mom's bedroom to find a pin. She kept this little, round glass milk jar on her dresser, filled with straight and safety pins, and stray buttons.

Something was missing. The photograph of my pretty young mother and my dashing young dad. Gone.

Mom must have put it away. I pricked my finger as I pinned my pants closed.

Mrs. McMahon, still in a fluffy pink bathrobe, waylaid me in the lobby. Through the small windows in the front door, I could see Dennis pacing in front of the Rolls, but her girth prevented me from opening it.

"Jake, I understand you're associated with that new musical *Suzy Q.*"

Did this woman pay informants? How else could she possibly dig up all of Carnegie Hill's gossip?

"I'm sorry, I'm late, Mrs. McMahon." I gestured toward the door. "Dennis is waiting . . ."

"Well, I thought you might be able to get me a couple of tickets for opening night. I just heard on the news that the show will go on."

I stared at her, deciding just how rude I could be and not have Mom kill me.

She must have taken my silence as assent. "And, Jake, when you find out where Elaine Eden is being waked, be sure and fill me in."

"Let me out of here, right now!"

To my surprise she opened the door, but then, as I walked out, she said, "Be a dear, Jake. You know how much my Patricia Ann loves culture. She deserves to attend an opening night. Can't you do a favor for your old neighbor?"

· · · · ·

By the time I collapsed in the cream-color leather seats in Dennis's convertible, I felt as if a steamroller had crushed my spirit. In five days, Mom would be married, moving to Washington, and visiting those cute pandas in the National Zoo. And I'd be left behind here in Manhattan, paying solitary visits to the seals in Central Park, and swallowing piles of horse manure from Mrs. McMahon.

"What's wrong with you, Jake?"

Had he read my mind? I'd bet that Modesty, at her most

miserable, had never felt as angry as I did on this glorious October morning. Or as confused. How could I have so totally lost my perky, positive attitude? Why was I wallowing in self-pity? I really did wish Mom and Aaron a wonderful life. Did I just hate change? Was I afraid to live alone? Actually, the prospect excited me. Could I be losing it? Going crazy?

"Nothing!" I snapped. "Why do you ask?"

"Maybe because I've known you forever and have loved you ever since you took a bite out of my hand." He placed his right hand—the one I'd bitten in an eight-year-old child's rage—over my left hand, and squeezed it. "Don't you know, if you want me, I'll always be here?"

I'd cry if I tried to speak, so I just nodded.

As the sun warmed the tops of our heads, we drove down Fifth Avenue. On the right, we passed the people sitting on The Metropolitan Museum of Art's steps, basking in the sunshine, the artists and booksellers who'd set up on the sidewalks in front of Central Park, the gold-and-red leaves on the trees behind them providing them with a magnificent backdrop, the entrance to the zoo, filled with small children, clinging to their parents' hands, and the elegant old Plaza Hotel, dazzling in the morning light.

By the time we reached Tiffany, the sights and sounds of the city I loved had cheered me up. And why not? I had the wind in my hair, a man who loved me holding my hand, and a murder to solve. What more could any woman want?

Twelve

Auturo Como, dressed in another Saville Row suit, grabbed my arm in the Globe's lobby. "I need to have a word with you, Jake. Alone."

Dennis shrugged, then smiled and stepped into the theater. Auturo led me into a small alcove next to an advance box office window, where his protruding stomach was seriously encroaching into my space.

"Yes?" What the hell did he want?

"We're trying to get back on track, Jake. Mulroney has promised me that we'll be able to open at the Baronet as scheduled. But he and his men are spread out like dog poop all over both the Baronet and the Globe. Questioning the cast, the musicians, the stagehands, the electricians, the wardrobe and makeup people, even the goddamn gofers. With the snail's pace this investigation is moving at, *Suzy Q* will never open on Thursday night!" He frowned, his thick brows meeting in the middle of the bridge over his broad, flat nose. "On the Lower East Side, where I grew up, we didn't trust cops. I still don't."

"Look, Mr. Como—"

"Auturo."

"Auturo. I'm sure the police are on top of things." I came off sounding prissy and pompous.

He didn't seem to notice. "Maybe, but I don't want to talk to them."

"You don't?"

"It would be a waste of time, Jake." He paused dramatically, then delivered his punch line. "You see, I know who killed Elaine."

I stared at him. "You do?"

"Yeah. And that's my problem. I don't want them arresting anyone connected with *Suzy Q*. Holding up our rehearsals."

Could this guy be for real? "Whoever cut that rope had to be connected with the show—"

"The hell you say. Elaine's airy fairy son, Tristan Hunter, wasn't part of my team, now, was he?"

At a loss for words, I waited.

"That heathen monk showed up here yesterday morning. Had a screaming match with Mommy. Are the cops focusing on that? No way! Mulroney's convinced my leading man's his boy. Sebastian James has browbeaten a broad or two in his time, but take my word for this, Jake, that big blowhard hasn't the balls to murder anyone."

I suspected Como's bottom line seriously colored that judgment call.

"You're a smart girl, Jake."

"At thirty-four, Auturo, I'm a woman—"

"You sure are, doll. Anyway, here's what I want to talk to you about. This murder is damn inconvenient."

The unmitigated gall of this guy. "I'm sure Elaine Eden would agree. . . ."

"Yeah." He lowered his eyes—narrow, slightly slanted, brown eyes, appearing even smaller in those deep pouches—just for a flicker, then met mine. "You see, Jake, Mulroney can't see the killer for the clues. And I think you can solve this case."

Such confidence. "Why would you think that?"

"Oh, come on, Jake. You've got something of a reputation, you know."

"Really?"

"Yeah. Dennis Kim told me how you solved those *Manhattan Magazine* critics' murders. Not that anyone in the business thinks that bastard Dick Peter didn't deserve to die. Some might say Elaine Eden did, too." Looking pensive, he rubbed his double chins. "I figure you can crack this case, too. And, from what I've heard about you, I'd bet you're already itching to try."

Damn Dennis. But how scary that Auturo could be so right about me. Most of my assignments, indeed, were murder. Some literally. And I did love being in the middle . . .

"I thought you could lead Lt. Mulroney in the right direction."

"And that would be away from the cast and crew . . ."

"All I ask is that you talk to Tristan. That is, if you can find him. Philip Knight gave me the number of the Leo House in Cheslea—that's where Tristan's staying—but he's not in his room. He hasn't checked out, though."

"Well, what's my priority, Auturo? Rewriting the script or tracking down Tristan?"

He smiled and his jowls shook like Jell-O. "I'm sure that a ghost as good as you are can do both without even rumpling your sheet."

I so hoped he'd turn out to be the one who killed Elaine, that I could prove it, that a jury would find him guilty, and that a judge would sentence him to life without possibility of parole. Still, I double-checked on the address of the Leo House, trying to ignore Auturo's grin.

Despite a strong police presence, the rehearsal had begun. I slipped into a seat in the last row and pulled my yellow legal pad and red pen out of my tote bag to take notes.

Eerily, they'd decided to pick up from right where Elaine Eden's Suzy Q had died. In a makeshift, very bare courtyard, with folding chairs in lieu of benches and no

Katmandu embassy standing behind them, Sebastian James's ambassador was greeting Morgan Drake, the new, very alive Suzy Q.

Dressed in the scarlet jumpsuit she'd worn yesterday, Morgan deftly disentangled herself from the rope ladder and stepped toward Sebastian. Since the Globe's stage was devoid of all scenery and, certainly, had no helicopter, I wondered why the rope ladder had been deemed a necessary prop.

Morgan kicked the ladder upstage, kissed Sebastian's cheek, and, in a booming voice, belted out the first lines of her opening number. Who knew? This beautiful woman could really sing. As she reached for, then grabbed the high C, closing the song with a wallop, even the cops applauded.

And she could act, too. Morgan and Sebastian projected a chemistry seldom seen on stage these days. Her old-fashioned sex appeal went way beyond suggestive dialogue, seductive looks, or steamy body language. Like the sirens of the silent screen days, she oozed sex . . . without saying a word. Somehow, she even made that old drunk has-been seem desirable. A major acting triumph.

By the middle of the scene, I'd put down my pad and pen and simply sat back and admired her performance.

"Grand, isn't she?" Philip Knight slid into the seat next to mine. "I'm Philip Knight, the director. I'm sorry we didn't get a chance to meet yesterday, Miss O'Hara."

I shrugged, "Well, under the circumstances . . ."

He nodded, then smiled wistfully. "Such a great tragedy. Elaine Eden was the light of my life. Dark despair now fills my empty soul."

Would that be why he kept on beaming every time Morgan Drake delivered a line?

"Aren't you supposed to be directing, Mr. Knight?"

"My job is done, Miss O'Hara. With a star as talented as Morgan Drake, the director can sit back and enjoy the show." He pointed to the blank page in my lap. "Like the ghostwriter."

"An amazing performance, I'd say. Almost a miracle. Tell me, Mr. Knight, was the understudy—er . . . —Peggy Malfa—as well prepared to step into the starring role as Morgan Drake was?"

"As well prepared, Miss O'Hara," he said smoothly, "but not half as talented."

"Then . . ."

"A director is often called upon to make extremely difficult decisions. Peggy Malfa is good—actually, she's great, but Morgan has star quality. No contest, Miss O'Hara. Mark my words, Morgan Drake will be big box office. A Broadway star in the tradition of Julie Andrews, Carol Channing, and Ethel Merman. Furthermore, Auturo Como, Sir Gareth Selby-Steed, and I all want—no, we need this show to be a hit. After all, that's the reason why you were brought on board, isn't it?"

"Right." I picked up the pad. "So I'd better get back to work."

"One more thing," he said. "I think I know who killed Elaine."

"Why don't you share that information with Lt. Mulroney?"

"Oh, I did, earlier, but he doesn't seem too interested in my theory. However, Dennis Kim overheard me talking to the detective and decided that you might be."

"Oh?"

"When act one is over, we'll take a break. I'd like you and Dennis to join Morgan and me for lunch at Sardi's."

"Only if I can sit under Angela Lansbury."

Philip Knight stood. "I'll make the reservation."

Thirteen

Leaving the Globe proved difficult. Tired, cranky, and fed up, I couldn't wait to get the hell out of the theater and lash out at bigmouthed Dennis Kim, who further frustrated me with his self-satisfied smile. Lt.Mulroney, now stationed in the lobby, intercepted our departure.

"Ms. O'Hara, right?" He sounded as weary as I felt. His tweed jacket looked rumpled, and he had dark circles under his blue eyes. Sleep-deprived and harried. I thought of Ben and how little sleep he'd gotten when working a homicide.

"Yes, Lt. Mulroney, Jake O'Hara." I extended my hand, good manners kicking in by reflex. Decades of my mother's etiquette lessons had left me better trained than Pavlov's dog.

Mulroney glanced at his notes. "And you're Dennis Kim, the attorney?"

Had I merely imagined the scorn in the detective's voice?

Maybe not. As Dennis acknowledged who and what he was, I noticed he was looking far less smug.

Mulroney said, "I'd like to schedule an interview with

you, Ms. O'Hara. Tomorrow morning?" He brushed several messy strands of brownish gray hair away from his eyes. "Nine-thirty, okay? Your place." He checked his notes again. "Carnegie Hill. Ninety-second Street. I'd rather talk to you away from here, and most people seem to prefer their homes to my station house."

I could understand that. "Nine-thirty's fine."

"You, too, Counselor. At your office." The detective flipped to another page in his notebook. "Thirty Rock, right? How's eleven-thirty? I should be able to make it back downtown by then."

"If it's okay with you, Lieutenant, I'd like to be present when you interview Ms. O'Hara." Dennis Kim's professional personality sparkled.

"Why? Does she need a lawyer?" Mulroney sounded less than charmed.

Enough of Dennis's interference! "I assure you I don't need an attorney, and, if I did, I wouldn't use Mr. Kim."

Mulroney's quick grin made him look a decade younger.

We finally left the theater. The morning sun had vanished and the temperature had dropped. Shivering, I turned up the collar on my blazer and jammed my hands into its pockets. Sardi's was only a short walk, but it would be a damn chilly one. Especially for Dennis.

"What the hell is the matter with you, Dennis? Why did you tell Auturo Como that I'd solved the *Manhattan Magazine* murders?"

"Because I knew he'd take the bait." Dennis laughed. "I'll bet Auturo served up a smorgasbord filled with clues, while trying to convince you that Tristan Hunter killed Elaine. Nothing like a little matricide to juice up a murder."

"Too Tall Tom is just as convinced that Tristan would never be capable of murdering his mother—or anyone else, for that matter."

"Aha! Is Elaine's son yet another one of Too Tall Tom's true loves? His first Buddhist, perhaps? Or maybe they knew each other eons ago, before Tristan Hunter's conversion? Because, for the last couple of decades, the monk has been off praying and fasting and not having sex in some remote region of Tibet."

"You're such a snake, Dennis. And not to be trusted. After you blabbed to Auturo, you went and told Philip Knight that I'd be interested in his theory!"

"Well, aren't you?"

"Does everyone connected with *Suzy Q* know I'm—"

"No." He wrapped an arm around me. "I haven't had time to tell them all."

I felt warmer or I would have pulled away from him. He snuggled closer yet. "Hey, I just wanted to jump-start your investigation, Jake. You want to do this. I can help. Don't look a gift horse in—"

"His goddamn big mouth."

He gently cupped the back of my neck, then kissed me on the lips, right in front of Sardi's.

Suddenly transported back to the Bridge of Sighs, I yearned to say yes.

"Is it because I'm divorced?" Where had that come from? And Dennis sounded dead serious. "Is that why you wouldn't marry me?"

I stared at him. Then I reached up, took his face in my hands, and kissed him.

"I've filed for an annulment, Jake. Wendy Wu never wanted kids, and said so in front of witnesses. Please tell your mother that, if you marry me, we can have a big church wedding in St. Thomas More's. We can have the cardinal over for dinner. And we can send all of our kids to Catholic schools."

"All?"

"Yeah. Two or three, anyway. You and I are only children. Wouldn't you like—"

I kissed him again.

"Public displays of affection are always so tacky," Sir Gareth Selby-Steed said as he scrambled past us and opened the door.

Sitting at the small bar near the entrance, Larry Cotter was keeping a young woman company while waiting for his lover. She held a martini in one hand and a wad of tissues in the other, alternating between gulping her drink and blowing her nose. A plain woman in her early thirties, with short, straight, no-nonsense hair, a narrow face, a well-shaped nose, and good skin. No makeup. Her eyes were red and swollen and, based on the size of the pile of tissues in her lap, I figured she'd been crying for some time. Her scarlet jumpsuit caught my attention. Exactly like Morgan's. Exactly like Elaine's.

"The missing understudy," Dennis whispered in my ear.

Sir Gareth introduced us. "Jake O'Hara, Dennis Kim, may I present Peggy Malfa, the talented lady who should be starring as our Suzy Q."

He almost sounded sincere. But from what Dennis had told me this morning, I had the impression that Sir Gareth Selby-Steed, not wanting to lose his investment, had readily gone along with the director's decision when Philip Knight had insisted on Morgan Drake taking over the lead.

"Jake's been rewriting my words," Larry explained to Peggy. "Of course, since she's a ghost, I get the credit. Like anyone gives a rat's—"

Sir Gareth snapped, "Get over it, Larry!"

"I'm pleased to meet you, Miss O'Hara. Mr. Kim," Peggy Malfa said, slurring ever so slightly.

I hadn't seen her or Larry at the theater. I bet they'd skipped rehearsal, and had been sitting in Sardi's, commiserating and getting quietly sloshed. Their presence certainly hadn't been required. Morgan had taken Peggy's place and I'd taken Larry's. What a lousy deal for both of them!

I wondered what time they'd arrived here. Where had they been earlier. Sardi's surely hadn't started serving booze at ten o'clock on a Sunday morning. Somehow I couldn't picture this pair in church. But then, you never knew. Most of all, why was Peggy wearing that jumpsuit? Unless . . .

"It's nice to meet you, too, Peggy. And please call me Jake. Er . . . —I'd like to . . . —well, my God, there's no polite way to ask this, so here goes—why are you in costume? Did you just find out this—"

"That's right, Jake," Peggy said, her voice cracking, "and aren't you the smarty-pants? A regular armchair detective. When I showed up at the Globe this morning and changed into my jumpsuit, Philip Knight told me that I would now be understudying Morgan Drake. And after all I'd—" She abruptly stopped talking and drained her glass.

"Jake, I have the table you requested. We're ready to order," Philip Knight called from behind me. Dennis and I said our good-byes to the understudy, the scriptwriter, and the composer, then moved on to the director and the star.

"So, what's his theory?" I asked Dennis as we followed Philip. With all that kissing and talking about raising a family, I'd become, understandably, sidetracked.

"Don't know." Dennis shrugged. "But, when I heard he had one, I thought of you."

As a diversion! It occurred to me that Dennis had been trying all morning—starting with my wake-up call—to get my mind off Mom's wedding, maybe off Modesty's, too, and on to murder. Then why had he brought up all that stuff about us getting married? Another diversion? Or . . .

Philip stopped short and I walked right into his back. "Oh! Sorry. Excuse me."

He said graciously, "Don't give it a thought, Jake. I guess we all have a lot on our minds. Please sit down."

I did. Directly under Angela Lansbury. And directly across the table from Morgan Drake.

Up close, the woman looked even more beautiful than on stage. All that dark hair, tumbling down around pale skin, and eyes so blue and so bright, I figured she had to be wearing contacts. No one's eyes could be that blue.

She gave me a megawatt smile. "Hi, Jake. I'm so glad we'll have a chance to get to know each other—even under these miserable conditions. Poor Elaine. What a dreadful way to go!"

I just nodded.

Then she turned her considerable charm on Dennis. "Of course, I've met Dennis. So great to see you again. And thank you for bringing Jake in to save *Suzy Q*. We're all ever so grateful."

Jesus, did the entire cast and crew know the show's producers had hired a ghost? Very unusual in my line of work.

Sardi's wait staff fussed over Philip Knight, who directed them to serve the first course, as they savored Morgan Drake, who ate up their attention.

Preferring diner food to gourmet, I resented Philip preselecting our menu, but since I wasn't hungry anyway, I'd concentrate on the bread, which was wonderful. However, when the soup arrived, I reevaluated . . . thick minestrone, absolutely delicious.

As Dennis made small talk, I also reevaluated Knight. Tan, tall, and lean, his hair streaked with silver, he had to be pushing seventy, but looked a decade younger. Dressed as if he'd just finished taping a *Lifestyles of The Rich and Famous* episode. Smooth and silky voice . . . like a seducer in a Victorian melodrama . . . or a telemarketer trying to sell you swampland in Florida.

Philip turned away from Dennis in midsentence, catching me in full appraisal mode, dissecting him.

"Jake, do I have soup on my chin? Or are you pondering what my murder theory might be. Several of my friends at *Manhattan* have told me how clever you are."

"Sorry if I seemed to be staring at you, Philip. My thoughts were actually in Florida." I heard Dennis stifle a chuckle. "And, yes, please do tell me about your theory."

"First, let me tell you how much I will miss my sweet Elaine." He wiped a dry eye. "Why, I couldn't sleep last night. The bed felt so empty . . . you know . . ."

Yeah, yeah. I knew. As empty as his soul, filled now only with dark despair. We'd played this scene earlier.

"Philip adored Elaine!" Morgan barely buttered a minuscule piece of Italian bread. "One of Broadway's greatest love stories."

A geriatric *Romeo and Juliet*. Favorably reviewed by the other woman. How touching.

I used my highly cultivated Irish wakes and funerals voice. "Well, Philip, try not to dwell on the past. I know you want to find your fiancée's killer. Let's talk about that theory."

"As the theater world is well aware, Sebastian James has been the bane of Elaine's existence for decades. A detestable drunk and a dangerous enemy."

"So you think her thrice ex-husband killed her?" Pretty unoriginal plot if you asked me.

"No." Philip rolled his eyes. A silent commentary on how dense he felt I was? "I believe that someone killed Elaine on Sebastian's behalf."

His theory had just become a hell of a lot more intriguing. "Really? Do you think he hired a hit man?"

"No, Jake, the murderer's motive was love."

Philip had me hooked. "Love?"

"Yes. Love. An Electra complex. Unnatural and unhealthy. Cynthia Malone dotes on Sebastian James. Fusses over him like a love-obsessed daughter. She would go to any lengths to please him. Just ask *Suzy Q*'s cast and crew."

I nodded.

"Why, at Barrymore's, on the night before the murder, she rescued him after he'd staged a boorish attack on Elaine." Philip sighed. A low, sad sigh.

No mention that Morgan Drake had made a quick exit from Barrymore's when Elaine Eden entered.

"An ugly drunken scene, Jake. Cynthia cleaned up after him, then got him out of there. And that was their pattern.

He made a mess. She fixed it. She worshiped him, for God's sake. Sick! She knew how much Sebastian hated Elaine. That he wanted her out of his life. So Cynthia Malone arranged for that to happen."

Fourteen

Act two didn't start till 3:00 P.M. I yawned in my seat in the last row of the orchestra. From exhaustion, not boredom. Standing, I stretched, and decided to go home. Grab a snooze. Then get in a couple hours of rewrites before tonight's dinner party at the River Café.

The changes might not be as dreadful as I'd anticipated. After Elaine had demanded that I rewrite Suzy Q as younger and sexier, I'd penciled in dialogue and attitude in an attempt to convey that image . . . and to try and make the audience believe it. Not easy turning a sixty-something into a siren. Now with a live one in the role—I snickered at my tasteless pun—the work should go much faster.

Ironic. I'd ghostwritten a book that starred a woman of a certain age as the sophisticated Suzy Q. A strong, smart, attractive, vital lady. A dream role for any older actress. Yet not good enough for the vain Elaine. Then today I'd watched Morgan Drake step in and play the part to perfection. Far better than her predecessor could have ever done.

I said good-bye to no one, just ducked out into the now much colder afternoon.

Dennis had left right after lunch, explaining he had to drive to Brooklyn to oversee last-minute arrangements for Mom and Aaron's party. He not only hadn't forgotten, apparently, he'd turned into a male Martha Stewart, about to host a night to remember.

On our brief walk from Sardi's back to the Empire theater, he hadn't brought "us" up again. His lawyer mentality? Not overstating your closing argument. Allowing the jury to ruminate on the salient points.

I, the jury, fantasized about an annulment, a church wedding, babies being baptized, and my mother, in ecstasy, playing Grandma. Aaron smiling warmly at her side.

Then Ben crashed my fantasy. Standing somewhat apart from the happy family. His eyes dark and sad.

Snapping back into reality, I hailed a cab. Why should I ride the Madison Avenue bus uptown? Auturo the Angel and Sir Gareth Selby-Steed could goddamn well pay for their ghost's transportation!

· · · · ·

Mom wasn't home. I'd better get used to that. But I had messages from both Modesty and Too Tall Tom. I played them back.

"Jake, this is Modesty. I'll be arriving late at Dennis Kim's party. Stop scowling." I laughed out loud. How well she knew me. *"I have a damn good reason. I called Cynthia Malone this morning. Told her I couldn't get her Gothic romance gook out of my mind—ugh—and that I'd run into an agent who might be interested in reading her manuscript. I know that's a miserable thing for one writer to do to another, but hell, all's fair in love and murder investigations, right? And it worked! She's meeting me at Barrymore's after the rehearsal. At six. I'll fill you in at the River Café. Rickie and I are taking a water taxi over there. We shouldn't be more than thirty minutes late. Ciao!"*

Too Tall Tom had been playing detective, too.

"If you're looking for Tristan, he's with me. Do you think I can bring him along to Dennis's soiree?"

Terse. The shortest message that my dear friend, usually a loquacious man, has ever left me. Where were they? Did Tristan know that everyone, including the police, wanted to talk to him?

I dialed Too Tall Tom's apartment. No answer. None on his cell phone, either. I left messages asking him to call me, advising him it was urgent that we speak, but not telling him yes, certainly, you can bring your old flame to the party. If he and Tristan were out on the town, I might not hear back for hours. Auturo's theory suddenly took on more weight. Could Too Tall Tom be entertaining a killer?

I lay on my bed, wondering if I should call Lt. Mulroney. Or Ben? Or Dennis? I closed my eyes. Just for a minute.

My mother's voice woke me up. "Darling, I know you must be exhausted, but it's almost five-thirty. If we're going to be on time for the party, you have to get dressed now."

I hopped in the shower, still groggy, and still debating if I should call Mulroney.

As I blow-dried my hair, I decided that if I didn't hear from Too Tall Tom before we left for the party, I'd tell Ben as soon as we arrived at the restaurant. Then my mother barged in to discuss what I planned on wearing. She'd been shopping.

. . . . .

Tucked under the Brooklyn Bridge, the River Café has long been considered one of the prettiest restaurants in the five boroughs. A favorite of Gypsy Rose's and Mom's. Whenever I had a decent-size advance, I'd bring them here for Mother's Day.

Each of the tables, covered in pale peach linen, had a vase filled with roses, in exactly the same shade of peach, and a candelabra holding tall cream-color candles. The china and silver sparkled like the lights of lower Manhattan that were twinkling through our window. A three-piece combo played "As Time Goes By." Dennis hadn't missed a beat.

Maura O'Hara sparkled, too. Dressed in a black velvet pantsuit, with wide legs and short, fitted jacket—a dramatic departure from her basic beige—her only jewelry, her engagement ring, a diamond solitaire, and a diamond brooch that Aaron had given her this afternoon while they were feeding the seals. He'd hidden it in a box of Cracker Jack.

Everyone looked great. The guys were all in tuxedos. Gypsy Rose wore shocking pink satin, knowing that, instead of clashing with her red hair, the color complemented it. Jane had on a new Donna Karan. The color of red wine. Spaghetti straps. Slinky and sexy.

Mom had surprised me with a new outfit, too. Pale green silk. "The same green as your eyes, Jake," she'd said. Sleeveless, with a Sabrina neckline, and a short, flippy skirt. Amazingly, it fit. She'd even bought me a pair of strappy high-heel sandals, so I felt I looked pretty hot myself.

I hoped nothing would ruin this glittering evening.

All of the lesser literary lights from Mom's Friday night salon had been invited. Our old friends from Jackson Heights, Linda and Mike Rogers, and their three sons were chatting with Mom. Dennis had arranged for our elderly neighbors the Neals to be picked up in a limo. Several members of my Ghostwriters Anonymous group were already on the small dance floor. Mr. Kim, who'd closed up shop, lindied with Jane.

"Do you think the wedding reception can top this?" Ben Rubin whispered in my ear as he put an arm around my waist and led me to the dance floor.

"I doubt it," I smiled up at him, shamelessly flirting.

"You're looking lovely tonight, Jake." No sooner had he spoken than the combo segued into "Just the Way You

Look Tonight." We both laughed, and Ben pulled me closer. His nose in my hair. In the background I could hear Dennis's baritone booming, *"Lovely, never never change . . ."*

I knew I had to tell Ben about Too Tall Tom and Tristan being among the missing, but just as I started to speak, Modesty's noisy arrival caught my attention, and I shut my mouth.

"Jake! Come over here, right this minute," she shouted from the door. "You won't believe what Cynthia Malone thinks!"

As I excused myself, Ben said, "Still playing Nancy Drew, Jake?" I felt as if the temperature had just dropped fifty degrees.

Modesty and I retreated to the ladies' room. "We have to stop meeting like this," she said. Coming from her, a woman who never joked, that could be considered a funny line.

"Before you start Cynthia's tale, I want to say how great you look. You know, I don't think I've ever seen your legs before."

"Hey, Jake, hate to disappoint you, but I *was* kidding about our clandestine meetings creating a problem," she deadpanned.

I'll be damned. Living with and loving Rickie Romero had resulted in this card-carrying miserable misogynist developing a sense of humor.

"Well, I don't mind losing you to Rickie. He got you out of those shrouds."

"Shrouds! I wear tunics. Monklike tunics. And I'm not changing my style." She glanced at herself in the mirror. Her light blue dress, a frothy concoction of cloudlike tiers, ended several inches above her knees. And her shoes were even flimsier than mine. A metamorphosis as dramatic as Kafka's. "Well, except for special occasions." She actually giggled. "Rickie spent most of the afternoon teaching me how to walk. He's so graceful."

A job requisite for cat burglars.

I stared down at my shoes. "Can he give me lessons, too, before my maid of honor gigs? Okay, now what about Cynthia?"

"She's convinced that Sebastian James is her long-lost father."

"Jesus! Why would she tell you that?"

"Because I asked her if she'd ever considered writing a book based on her own life experiences. And, of course, I'd praised her Gothic gook to the hilt, so she felt all warm and fuzzy about me."

I smiled. Maybe Modesty hadn't changed, after all.

"What led Cynthia Malone to this bizarre conclusion?"

"She's adopted. Her American parents—both are now dead—had brought her over here from somewhere in the British Isles. And she's about the same age as the daughter Sebastian deserted when he ran off with Elaine. That poor little kid whose mother then committed suicide."

"But . . . there must be lots of adopted women who'd fit that vague profile. Besides, I think Mom told me that the maternal grandparents had raised Sebastian James's daughter."

"Cynthia really is a frosted flake. But you're right. Even if she bought my warm and fuzzy routine, why did she tell me this crazy story?"

"Why indeed? The woman barely knows you."

Modesty shrugged. "Beats me. Anyway, after two years researching on the Internet, Cynthia flew over to Britain and checked out hospital and birth records, orphanages, and adoption agencies. Claims that after her grandmother had died, her grandfather gave her up for adoption. Though she hasn't told Sebastian yet, she has proof that he's her father. Says that I'm absolutely bloody right: Her story will make a great book . . . and a blockbuster movie!"

. . . . .

As I sat down at the table, my mother asked, "Where is Too Tall Tom, darling?" She craned her neck, scouting out the room.

"Sorry, I forgot to tell you, he left a message—" I stopped dead. What could I say? That Too Tall Tom wanted to bring Tristan Hunter along as his date? That he hadn't returned my calls? That our dear friend might be off God only knows where, doing God only knows what with Elaine Eden's son, the Buddhist monk—who might have murdered his mother? How much of this pale imitation of a Greek tragedy did I want to reveal?

"And?" Mom sounded puzzled.

"And . . . —er . . . —he's going to be late." She didn't need to hear any of this. Not now. Hopefully, not ever.

"Should we start to eat or should we wait for him?" In the candlelight, my mother's face glowed, looking happy and beautiful.

"Let's eat!" I drained my champagne glass and glanced over at the dance floor. Gypsy Rose and Dennis were doing a tango. I smiled, thinking back to the night that Dennis had taught me to tango. What a glorious, sexy dance. I considered cutting in, but rejected the idea. Awed at how well they danced together, I just sat back and enjoyed the show.

The first course, the biggest shrimp cocktail that I've ever seen, arrived just as the dance ended, and Gypsy Rose and Dennis returned to the table, to the applause of all the other guests.

Dennis, probably just to be perverse, had placed Ben between Modesty and Jane, and as far away from me as possible.

"It's the host's prerogative to sit next to the prettiest woman at his table," he said, sotto voce, as he sat down.

"Hush."

"Why?" Dennis grinned. "I want the whole world to know."

"Know what, dear?" my mother asked.

But it was Gypsy Rose, apparently having a psychic

moment, who spoke. "We have a visitor at our table."

I held my breath. Gypsy Rose's contacts in the world beyond showed up at the damnedest times.

My mother asked, "Who is it?"

My cell phone rang.

Distracted from her curiosity regarding the uninvited ghost guest's identity, my mother said, "Jake, that's rude, darling, turn it off!"

"Excuse me, but I'd better answer it." I stood up. "It might be Too Tall Tom." I walked away as I pressed the On button. "Hello?"

"Thank God!" It was Too Tall Tom and he sounded frantic.

"What's wrong?"

"The world as I know it has fallen apart. That's what's wrong."

"Could you be a tad more specific?"

"Tristan is dead and the police seem to think I killed him!"

Fifteen

Every cliché that I've ever read—or written—happened to me all at the same time: My legs turned to rubber; my heart skipped a beat; my mouth went dry . . . as it dropped.

"Jake?" Too Tall Tom yelled into my right ear.

Afraid that he might be in custody, I asked, "Where are you?"

"Actually, I'm in a cab, crossing the Brooklyn Bridge, on my way to the River Café."

"I gather Tristan isn't along for the ride."

"You sound as mean as Modesty. That's neither the least bit funny nor the least bit compassionate. I've been through hell. That Detective Mulroney must have trained with the KGB. I've been grilled to a crisp. Fried. Drained . . ."

"Exactly where and when did Tristan die?" I adored Too Tall Tom, but he had this tendency to focus on his own point of view rather than laying out the facts up front.

"Turn left, driver . . . yes . . . head toward the river. Look, Jake, I'm almost there. Have a double Stoli on the rocks ready for my arrival!"

Feeling dazed, confused, and puzzled, I walked to the open bar and ordered his drink.

Gypsy Rose interrupted me as I headed back to the table, put her arm around my shoulder, and said, "It's Too Tall Tom, isn't it?"

I didn't even bother to inquire how she knew, confident that all would be revealed.

"I have a message for you from our unexpected guest, James Hilton . . ."

"Lost Horizon." I had to chuckle, thinking his Shangri-la was probably only a short mountain climb away from Tristan's monastery. And how far were either of those places from Katmandu, Nepal? My geography left much to be desired. "Did Zelda Fitzgerald send James Hilton?"

"She came along and introduced him to me. Such an articulate man—speaks like he writes."

"What did he say?"

"That he regretted missing you." Gypsy Rose sounded nervous, but obviously thrilled by her encounter with the author. "Jake, James Hilton is Tristan Hunter's spirit guide! He told me that Tristan is dead. And that Too Tall Tom is in trouble."

Nodding, I sighed, "I just got off the phone with Too Tall Tom." I raised the glass of vodka. "He'll be here any second now. This drink is for him."

"Then you're aware that Tristan has been murdered?"

"Yes. And the police seem to think Too Tall Tom murdered him!"

Gypsy Rose released me. "My God! We must speak to Ben. James Hilton's message was for you, but it came straight from Tristan. A clue to his killer."

"Tell me!"

"Tristan Hunter told James Hilton that—and I quote— 'it's all in the family.' "

" 'All in the family'? What does that mean?"

She stared at me, her dark green eyes troubled. "I have no earthly idea."

"Well, earth to the world beyond, Gypsy Rose! Channel

James Hilton! Get him back here. Ask him!"

"What kind of a psychic do you think I am? I asked him. He didn't know, either."

"Well, if he's Tristan's spirit guide, can't he—"

"Tristan is in transition. Can't be reached."

"Well, can't James or Zelda e-mail him or something?"

Gypsy Rose smiled. "Jake, they assured me that you would figure it out yourself!"

"Yeah. Well, it's comforting to know that the world beyond believes in me." I switched the Stoli from one hand to the other. The icy glass had turned my palm red and cold. "What family could Tristan have been talking about? He was an only child. His father, Brock Hunter, has been dead for years. His mother was just murdered. So who? A distant cousin?"

Gypsy Rose scrunched up her face. "Well, consider this, darling. Tristan may have no blood kin, but what about Sebastian James, his former stepfather and a current prime suspect? He could be considered *family*, couldn't he?"

A sharp signal in the back of my mind jolted me. I can't say the message came from the world beyond, but its delivery presented me with another, even more intriguing, possibility. "As could his former stepsister, Sebastian James's daughter."

Gypsy Rose pointed toward the door. "Oh, there's Too Tall Tom!"

As I turned to greet him, my mother stood abruptly, left the table, and joined us. "Thank God you're here," she said, as Too Tall Tom bent to kiss her cheek. "I was getting worried. Will all of you please sit down? They're about to serve the beef Wellington!"

Then Too Tall Tom, Gypsy Rose, and I communicated, without words, but with expressions that said it all. *Why ruin Maura's party? Don't discuss anything now. What difference will an hour or two make? Murder can wait till after dessert.*

I just hoped Lt. Mulroney wouldn't call Ben Rubin before the baked Alaska was served.

Carefully pushing the pâté away from the crust, I wound up with only a dab of roast beef and a bit of crust on my fork. Why was I being so damn fussy when, for once, I had so little appetite? I glanced up quickly to see if my mother had caught me messing around with my food—a cardinal sin in her etiquette book—and, instead, saw Dennis smiling and shaking his head.

He asked, "Enjoying the pâté, Jake? I understand it came straight from France."

My mother turned away from Aaron, her eyes scanning my plate. If I had my way, our waiter would serve Dennis's head on a platter along with the dessert.

The band was playing a melody of Broadway show tunes to dine by. "Come on, Ben," I said, after walking the length of the table, and extending my hand to him. "I'd rather dance than eat."

"Something on your mind, Jake?" Ben whirled me around to "The Sound of Music."

Maybe I'd grown sick of playing detective, tired of keeping secrets, fed up with a private and professional life that kept me crazed—or, maybe, I simply craved Ben Rubin's advice. For whatever reason, I told him everything, starting with Tristan's death and working backward to three nights ago at the Waldorf when I'd signed on as ghostwriter. The band had played several selections from *Carousel* and moved on to the score of *South Pacific* by the time I'd finished.

Ben seemed well aware of much of what I was reporting about the case. Nodded in empathy when he heard my concerns. Smiled when I told him about how two of the suspects had boldly fingered two other fellow suspects. I figured that he'd been staying in close touch with Mulroney.

"You're such a damn good investigator, Jake, that I hate to ask you to stop . . ."

"But, you are."

"For your own good." His hand tightened on the small of my back. "This is a dangerous game that you're playing. And I'm much too fond of my future stepsister to take a chance on losing her."

Now I wished I'd eaten my words along with the pâté. "But, Ben—"

"No buts. I'll drive you and Too Tall Tom home. He can tell us what happened . . . and I'll talk to Mulroney. That's the final curtain for you, Jake. Go back to your ghostwriting. Enjoy these last few days with your mother. Maybe even think about what you want to do with the rest of your life. A few of your close friends would like to know. Then for God's sake, let Midtown North's homicide department do their job."

To the tune of "I'm Gonna Wash That Man Right Outa My Hair," Ben and I returned to the table.

Observing the dinner guests exchange banter and smiles, I found it surprising that no one seemed to be aware of Too Tall Tom's distress.

If Mom knew something was up, she certainly gave no sign. And after the last bite of baked Alaska had been finished, and the last one of Dennis's, Mr. Kim's, and Gypsy Rose's speeches had come to an end, and Mom and Aaron had given their gracious thanks, she never blinked when Ben and I excused ourselves, saying that Too Tall Tom wasn't feeling well and we had to drive him home.

Dennis, however, did notice. As we said our good-byes, he whispered in my ear, "If Ben can't fix whatever is wrong, call me." Then he pulled Too Tall Tom aside for what I presumed must be advice and counsel.

My mother waved us off. "Don't worry, Dennis will drive Aaron and me home."

Hard to believe that we'd escaped from the River Café without a Maura O'Hara inquisition!

Sixteen

Except for an occasional comment on the party, the upcoming weddings, or the weather, we rode in silence as Ben drove across the Brooklyn Bridge and straight to Too Tall Tom's Christopher Street duplex.

The recently redecorated apartment reflected the owner's excellent craftsmanship and flair for interior design. The brick building, a recent landmark, ran narrow and deep, but a combination of rich color and impeccable taste had turned each of the condo's small rooms into a jewel box. I'd shared many a cup of tea with my best friend in the golden sunroom where the three of us now sat, each armed with a Stoli on the rocks.

Our host, who'd been far too quiet, finally opened up. "That cop Mulroney thinks I killed Tristan Hunter, Ben."

"Why?" Ben took a sip from his drink, then carefully placed his glass down on the sterling silver coaster that Too Tall Tom had handed him. A good sign, I thought. Our host might be frantic. But not so frantic that he wouldn't fuss over the possibilty of someone marring his Hepplewhite table.

"Well, among other things, I'm convinced that Mulroney is a homophobe. All that macho tough talk and with a former prizefighter's banged-up face to match. Then, too, I had just discovered the body as the coppers came bounding into Tristan's hotel room. And, unfortunately, I was holding the murder weapon in my hand!"

I almost knocked over my vodka. "But how?"

Ben said, "Why don't you start at the beginning? And, for your information, John Mulroney came out of the closet almost a decade ago. You can't judge a cop by his cover."

"Sorry," Too Tall Tom said. "I hate it when someone stereotypes me; now I'm guilty of doing the same thing."

"We've all done that at one time or another," I said, as Ben nodded. "Go on, tell us what happened today."

"Well, I met Tristan at Tavern on the Green. Considering that he'd just lost his mother, our lunch seemed quite festive. It occurred to me that his mourning period had been extremely brief."

"Yeah," I said, "like less than twenty-four hours."

Too Tall Tom sighed. "The only regret Tristan expressed was that Philip Knight had taken over the funeral arrangements and had allowed him no say in the matter."

Ben said, "Knight wasn't married to Elaine, and Tristan was her son, so why—"

"Elaine had made Philip executor of her will . . . and had given him power of attorney. Even though he'd taken a vow of poverty, Tristan had counted on inheriting his mother's money, but as of yesterday, that seemed to be in question."

"So," I said, "did you think he might have killed his mother?"

"No." Too Tall Tom drained his glass. "However, I do think he wanted to exit that Buddhist monastery, posthaste, and return to live in America. And that he felt no sorrow about Elaine's death—only that he might not be her heir."

Ben asked, "Where did you two go after lunch?"

"We split. He'd announced that he planned to meet with

Sir Gareth Selby-Steed after the rehearsal." Too Tall Tom
sounded angry. "Then, bold as brass, Tristan told all the
dirty details of an affair he'd had with Gareth years ago.
Seems he'd left the order for six months just before being
ordained. Had cold feet about taking his final vows, you
see. Traveled to London—'to experience life again'—met
Gareth at a club, and they had a fling. But then Tristan
caught his lover cheating on him. So he reconsidered his
options, rediscovered his vocation, and returned to the
monastery."

Too Tall Tom wiped his eyes with a linen cocktail napkin. "Those words that Tristan had spoken, so cavalierly,
devastated me. I jumped up and left him sitting at the
table, sipping his café au lait. Stuck him with the check!
Then I went down to see *I Love Lucy* at the Museum of
Broadcasting. You know how that show always cheers me
up, Jake."

Smiling, I said I knew.

"I'd forgotten to take my cell phone—which is like
another appendage—along with me to the Tavern on the
Green. I was that excited at the thought of being with
Tristan. Funny what a difference a day makes. Overnight,
my sweet, unassuming monk had morphed into a grasp-
ing, conniving man."

"I wondered why you hadn't returned my calls."

"Sorry, darling. When I returned home—around six-
thirty—I had two messages from you. One on the cell,
one on the regular phone. And a hysterical message from
Tristan. He said I must dash right over to the Leo House . . .
that Sebastian James had threatened to kill him . . . that he
took him at his word . . . that his former stepfather was on
his way there to murder him . . . Tristan begged me to
come . . . because of what we'd once meant to each other."

I reached over the coffee table to pat my best friend's
hand. A real stretch from my perch on the amber Queen
Anne chair to the aquamarine silk sofa, where Too Tall
Tom sat next to Ben. "And, of course, you went . . ."

He groaned, "*Mais oui!* You can never get a cab on Sunday night in the Village, and this evening was no exception. Then the subway took forever to come. I didn't get there soon enough!"

Ben said, "So when you arrived, you found Tristan's body. Is that right?"

Too Tall Tom nodded. "Dead in his bed."

I asked, "How did you get up to his room? Obviously Tristan didn't answer the front desk clerk's call to announce you."

"The Leo House isn't the Plaza, Jake!" Too Tall Tom almost, but not quite, chuckled. "As you know, I'd lived there years ago. And I visited only yesterday with Tristan. Spent some time up in his room, under very different circumstances, I must say!" This time a chuckle did escape, and he blushed before continuing. "Anyway, nuns man the desk. There are lots of young European guests, with backpacks, mingling with older clergymen from the Midwest. The place reminds me of the old Chelsea, before the lawyers and the investment bankers took over the neighborhood. All very casual. I walked into the lobby, the desk clerk, an elderly nun—or some poor soul who should have been one—was occupied with a young Frenchman's registration form, so I just dashed up the two flights of stairs to Tristan's room. I found the door ajar and I went right on in."

"How had he been killed?" I heard the tremor in my voice, feeling relieved that this was one corpse I hadn't stumbled upon.

"His head had been bashed in. Brains and blood all over the sheets. Ghastly sight. Poor Tristan. No one deserves such a dreadful end."

Ben asked, "And the weapon?"

"Elaine's Oscar. The killer had propped it up on the pillow, next to Tristan's bloody head. Next to his open wound. Obscene."

Jesus! Murdered with his mother's Academy Award!

"What then?" Ben asked.

I walked over to the bar and poured us each another drink.

Too Tall Tom was shaking his head. "I can't tell you why—there's no sane explanation, even for a film buff—but I picked up that Oscar and read the inscriptions: 'Best Actress. Elaine Eden. *Bitter Victory*. 1973.' Then the cops came charging through the door. With Sebastian James right behind them. And there I stood, with that goddamn Oscar in my hand. And Tristan's head still oozing blood."

. . . . .

Too Tall Tom, exhausted, said he had to go to bed. So we left. But not before Ben promised that he would talk to Mulroney and vouch for Too Tall Tom's sterling character, while steering Midtown North's investigation back to Sebastian James and why he had threatened to kill his former stepson. Sir Gareth Selby-Steed, Tristan's ex-lover, might have a motive as well. Ben and I had both wondered what those two might have been discussing this afternoon, just prior to the murder.

Now in the car, I fumbled, trying to buckle my seat belt. Feeling edgy. Tongue-tied. Concerned about Too Tall Tom, but almost as concerned about being alone with Ben.

We drove in silence. East past Washington Square Park, then north on First Avenue, heading for the entrance to the FDR Drive. A mixed neighborhood. Crack dealers operating out of a deserted tenement on one block. A movie star's loft on the next.

Damn! I couldn't deal with yet another silent car ride. If we couldn't talk about our feelings, by God, we could talk about facts. At this moment, I would prefer to discuss the case rather than our love life—or lack thereof—and I figured Ben would, too.

"Why do you think Mulroney didn't drag Too Tall Tom down to Midtown North for questioning?"

"Well, they grilled him at the scene, so either Mulroney doesn't think Too Tall Tom killed Tristan, or doesn't think he has enough evidence, or suspects someone else."

"But for God's sake, Ben, he had the bloody murder weapon clutched in his hand!"

"John Mulroney's a film buff, too. Always quoting from Hitchcock movies. I swear he knows every line of dialogue from *The Birds*. Maybe he believed Too Tall Tom when he explained how he couldn't resist picking up the Oscar."

"Come on," I said, "even I had trouble believing that!"

"And Homicide will check out the Sebastian James angle. Just because he arrived right behind the uniforms doesn't mean that he hadn't arrived there earlier, bopped Tristan, waited somewhere—like the stairwell—then acted shocked to discover Tristan dead, and Too Tall Tom looking guilty."

"Right. Maybe someone had seen Sebastian in the lobby, before Tristan arrived. Or what about phone records?"

"If Sebastian James had indeed phoned Tristan, and Tristan then called Too Tall Tom, that would help prove . . ."

What was he thinking? "Ben, you don't doubt that's exactly what happened, do you?"

"Hey, what I think doesn't matter. This is Midtown North's case, not mine. But a story always sounds so much better when the investigation turns up some proof to collaborate it."

Story? Would Ben be going to bat for Too Tall Tom with Mulroney if he didn't have total faith in him? I was tired and upset. After all, I had trouble understanding how Too Tall Tom could have grabbed that Oscar. Ben's just being a cop—and cops are very different from . . .

As if by mutual consent, we remained silent for the rest of the trip. When we arrived at Ninety-second Street, Ben hopped out of the car and opened my door before I had my seat belt off. Then he grabbed me, pulled me to him, and kissed me. My toes danced. So did my heart.

Finally ready to speak, I opened my eyes and spotted

Dennis's Rolls-Royce pulling up next to Ben's car.

Damn! He must have driven Mom and Aaron home.

As I struggled to extricate myself from Ben's arms, Dennis stepped out of the driver's seat, and waved at me.

Seventeen

I'd clocked into bed at 12:30 A.M. and out of bed at 8:00 A.M., but those numbers didn't add up to anything resembling a good night's sleep.

Tossing and turning, I'd thought about Ben and Dennis. Right after *the kiss*, Mom and Aaron had stepped out of Dennis's Rolls, but, apparently, had missed the moment. Just as well. Dennis, on the other hand, hadn't missed a thing. His smirk kept reappearing all night. So did Ben's wry grin, making me wonder if I should start searching for bachelor number three. Then, suddenly, both images would vanish, only to be replaced with the memory of Elaine crumpled in a heap on stage right and Too Tall Tom telling me about discovering Tristan dead in bed! These grim scenes were followed by nagging questions about possible suspects and probable motives.

The deaths had to be connected. So had the killer always planned to kill Tristan as well as Elaine? Or, after his mother's murder, had the son discovered something that made him dangerous? If Tristan had been on the killer's wish list—along with Elaine—who, among the suspects, knew that he had been planning to return to New York City?

Sebastian James's threat intrigued me. Why call and warn your prospective victim? Calling would erase any element of surprise, so crucial to a killer. Why not just show up, catch him off guard, then bop him one with the Oscar? More likely that big ham just wanted to scare Tristan. But why? Trying to get him to leave town? Could Sebastian have been trying to help Cynthia Malone? To protect her from whatever Tristan might have known about his mother's murder. If, that is, he'd actually known something. Could Tristan have seen Cynthia cut the ladder's ropes? She'd certainly had both the means and opportunity. Her motive? Maybe revenge for Elaine having stolen her father away from her? Possible. Paying Elaine back for mistreatment of her father for all these years? Seemed rather flimsy. Unless Cynthia turned out to be even crazier than I suspected.

Why did Tristan have his mother's Oscar in his room? Had she given it to him? Did he always travel with it? Kind of a heavy weight to take globe-trotting. And knowing how vain Elaine Eden had been, I would have thought she'd have wanted to display her Academy Award on a mantelpiece.

And what about Tristan's afternoon meeting with Sir Gareth Selby-Steed? Had the songwriting knight returned later that evening? Could their romance in London all those years ago have any connection to Tristan's murder tonight? Could Sir Selby-Steed have been acquainted with Elaine Eden long before she'd been cast as Suzy Q?

I'd been wide awake when the alarm went off. And damn grateful to have a reason to get out of bed.

Though I'd updated Mom before going to bed last night, I'd abridged the part about Too Tall Tom being the prime suspect. She deserved a good night's sleep. Aaron could fill her in today.

Now I put water on to boil and popped a cinnamon raisin bagel in the toaster oven. When the phone rang, I grabbed it fast, not wanting to disturb Mom's rest.

"Ms. O'Hara?" a woman with a Bronx accent asked.

"Yes, this is Jake O'Hara."

"Lt. Mulroney asked me to call. He won't be able to meet with you at nine-thirty. But he said he'll see you later at the Globe."

"Thanks." I glanced over at the kitchen clock and hung up, smiling. Mulroney would have been stood up. I'd forgotten all about our scheduled interview.

· · · · ·

Well before nine, I was standing on a crowded Fifth Avenue bus heading downtown. I'd get off at Forty-forth Street and walk the few blocks west to the theater. The rehearsal wouldn't start till ten, so I'd have time to rewrite in peace.

But at Forty-sixth Street, I checked my watch—9:20. Maybe I'd just stay on the bus. Ride down to Chelsea. Pay a quick visit to the Leo House. Ask the desk clerk a few questions.

On Eighth Avenue and Twenty-third Street, Chelsea looked pretty much unchanged. Trendy as the rest of the neighborhood had become, the same old coffee house on the southeast corner was still doing a thriving business. And the passersby—except for a few tourists—looked like those rarest of the city's residents, native New Yorkers.

· · · · ·

Spartan understated the Leo House lobby's decor. Behind the counter, a small older woman, dressed in navy blue polyester, nervously ran her stubby fingers through iron gray hair. In front of the counter, two young men, hardly out of their teens, and a young woman—all wearing black T-shirts, jeans, and down vests—juggled their backpacks, while gesticulating wildly and speaking loudly in a foreign language. Russian, I thought.

It looked as if it might be a long registration process.

Then a tall, toned, tawny-haired exotic creature emerged from the elevator. She wore a leather jumpsuit that matched her beautiful hair and carried a motorcycle helmet. Also in earth tones. Greeting the three prospective guests with kisses on both cheeks, she then translated for them with gusto. In no time, the new arrivals had their keys and were following Wonder Woman up to their rooms.

As the clerk was finishing her paperwork, I seized the moment.

"Hi, my name's Jake O'Hara and I'm a writer."

In situations like this, I've discovered that sticking as close as possible to the truth gave me a distinct advantage. Modesty, on the other hand, always preferred to use the most outrageous cover story that she could conjure up.

"Yes, did you want a room, dear?" The older lady gave me a warm smile. "If you did, I'm afraid we're all filled up." She sighed flipping through the registration book. "Not a thing available till October twenty-fourth. And then only with a shared bath."

"How many people would share that bath?" I was really curious.

"Two to four. That would only apply to the shower and tub. Of course, even our rooms with shared baths come equipped with their own sinks and commodes."

I smiled back, appreciating her refinement and the use of that old-fashioned word.

"You've never stayed at the Leo House?"

"No . . . but a dear friend of mine lived here for a while." She nodded. Now or never. I plunged. "You see, it was his friend, Tristan Hunter, who—er—died here yesterday."

She actually recoiled, stepping back away from the counter, as if trying to escape from me. "Did you say you were a writer? What newspaper do you work for?" All warmth had evaporated.

"I'm a ghostwriter. Books, mostly." I glanced at her name tag—Agnes Carroll. "Look, Ms. Carroll—"

"It's Miss."

"Sorry, *Miss* Carroll. I just want to ask you a couple of questions. Off the record. The police seem to think my friend had something to do with Tristan Hunter's death." My voice broke. "I promise you that he didn't. He's a good and gentle soul. I think the murdered man might have had another visitor yesterday afternoon . . . before my friend arrived. Were you on duty?"

"Yes. And the police asked me that same question."

I waited.

"Well, I guess it wouldn't hurt to tell you . . ."

I nodded.

"Mr. Hunter brought that Englishman back with him. The one who writes those Broadway musicals. Selby-Steed. Excuse me, *Sir* Selby-Steed. The Leo House doesn't get many British knights, you know. I recognized him right off. I've certainly seen that fat moon-face often enough in the newspapers and on television."

"What time would that have been?"

"Around six. I get off at seven on Sundays. I didn't see him leave. It can get pretty hectic here, and I might not have noticed, but I don't think so."

"My friend didn't arrive until later . . ."

"He's the one who found the body, isn't he?"

"Right." I sensed her revulsion. No doubt she was well aware that Too Tall Tom had been caught with the murder weapon in his hand. "Miss Carroll, did anyone else ask for Tristan Hunter yesterday? Maybe a tall young woman with dark hair?"

Agnes Carroll smiled. "Most young women are tall compared to me, Miss O'Hara. But no one, tall or short, asked for Mr. Hunter while I worked the desk yesterday."

"Well, maybe she'd been hanging around the lobby?"

Miss Carroll shook her head, then ran those tiny fingers through her hair again. "Wait . . . I almost forgot—there was a woman! And I think she did have dark hair. Yes, I'm sure she did. She came through the lobby twice. The first time around five or so. Went straight to the elevator.

I figured that she must have known where she was going, probably had the room number, but then I saw her again about an hour later."

"This is very important. What did she look like?"

"Well, she had on big oversized sunglasses, so I didn't see much of her face. A dark jacket. Fleece, I think. Jeans. Sneakers? Maybe, maybe not. Slim. But I don't think she was tall." Miss Carroll gave her hair a final pat. "Her behavior did strike me as a bit odd, but why are you asking questions about her? Do you think she could have been involved in Mr. Hunter's death? Who is this woman?"

"That's what I'd like to know!" Lt. John Mulroney's loud voice startled me.

Eighteen

Mulroney led me out the back door and into a small sunlit garden. But at 9:30 on this crisp fall morning, despite the sun, the air felt chilly. Several guests, mostly young, hearty Nordic types, had carried their cafeteria-style plastic trays into the garden, and were seated at two of the tiny round tables, enjoying their cereal and bananas al fresco.

Gesturing to a table well removed from the tourists, Mulroney said, "Sit down, Jake. I guess destiny has determined that I'm doomed to interview you at nine-thirty this Monday morning. Who am I to fight fate? I'm going to get a cup of coffee. Want one?"

"Thanks. But I'd rather have tea. No sugar. Not much milk. I like it kind of dark."

As he headed inside to the self-service dining room, I heard him sigh.

I thought about what he would ask me and, more importantly, how I would respond. Tell all? Well, that certainly wasn't an option! But I could reveal enough to entice him to lay off Too Tall Tom and to check out Cynthia Malone and Sir Selby-Steed.

Cold, I turned my brown tweed jacket's collar up. Itchy. And I was still cold. Autumn in New York. Why hadn't I worn a lightweight coat over my jacket? Or at least carried one with me?

"Is this to your liking?" Mulroney placed a cup of tea in front of me. More dark than light, and looking exactly how I liked it.

"Yes. Thanks."

He sat and stared at me. His eyes so alive, in sharp contrast to his weary, lined face. "Ben Rubin tells me you suffer from a severe case of Nancy Drew syndrome. The last young woman I ran across with that diagnosis died, suddenly and most unpleasantly.

"But the original is alive and well and she's been around for the better part of a century."

He never cracked a smile.

I sipped my tea, then tried a new tack. "Look, Lt. Mulroney, the reason I'm consumed with Nancy Drew fever is because you seem to think that my best friend killed Tristan Hunter."

"I'd be interested in hearing who you think killed him. And his mother, too. Every Nancy needs a Ned to confide in. Don't you consider me perfect for the role?"

Though I couldn't even get him to smile, he made me laugh out loud. "An exchange of information requires dialogue, Ned."

"Start with a monologue, Jake, and we'll see how the scene plays."

So I told him. All about how Cynthia Malone claimed to be Sebastian James's long-lost daughter, and how I believed that she'd shown up here early last evening, wearing sunglasses and a dark jacket, attempting to blend in with the other guests. All about Sebastian's verbal abuse of Elaine Eden, how he'd hated her for decades, and how I hadn't even had a chance to ask Miss Carroll if she'd seen Sebastian James last evening before the murder, because he—Mulroney—had interrupted me. All about Sir Gareth Selby-Steed's long-ago affair with Tristan, and how he'd arrived at six and spent a good chunk of time up in Tristan's room, despite the fact that he had a current lover, Larry Cotter. All about how Philip Knight had turned out to be the executor—and probable heir—of Elaine's estate and how he'd been romancing the second lead, Morgan Drake, while engaged to Elaine, and how he'd given his squeeze the starring role after Elaine's death, making the understudy, Peggy Malfa, very angry. All about how Auturo Como was in debt up to his double chins and how he'd collect on an act of God insurance policy he'd taken out on Elaine Eden. All about how Sir Gareth Selby-Steed would share in that bounty. All about how the producer and the composer had hated the star and had wanted her out of the show. And, finally, all about my theory that Tristan might have stumbled onto his mother's killer's identity and that's why he'd been murdered, too.

By the time I finished, he'd had two more coffees, I'd had another tea, and we'd each had a jelly doughnut.

He had only one comment on my soul-baring, and sharing almost everything I knew about the case: "I don't like that pompous ass Sebastian James, either. He actually told me that Cynthia Malone's not good-looking enough to be his daughter."

Talk about taking the wind out of my sails! "So you knew about Cynthia claiming to be Sebastian's daughter!"

"Jake O'Hara, regardless of what misguided notions you may have, I assure you that Midtown North's Homicide Department has solved a good number of cases without Nancy Drew's help. It's annoying to me, but it could be fatal for you. So you listen up. Butt out. Or, I promise, I'll charge you with obstructing justice. I'll bring you in for questioning on Friday evening. You might even miss your mother's wedding."

Then he stood and walked away without saying goodbye. I cleaned up the cups and paper plates, convinced that John Mulroney was no Ned.

. . . . .

As I entered the Globe, Morgan Drake stood onstage
aiming a gun at Sebastian James. Of course, the script
called for Suzy Q to not recognize the ambassador and,
mistakenly, shoot him in the arm, thinking he was one of
the bad guys.

Larry Cotter scurried up the aisle and into the last row,
taking the seat next to mine, stretching out his long legs
under the seat in front of him. Actually, they were spread
over two rows.

"Why do you always sit so far in the back, Jake? I can
hardly hear the dialogue."

"Pity the paying customers. At over one hundred bucks
a ticket, they won't be able to hear, either."

"The acoustics are much better at the Baronet. We'll be
back there tomorrow. In the meantime, why don't we
move down to seventh row center. Auturo and Gareth are
there. And they may have some suggestions."

I gave him a big warm smile, then spoke firmly. "Larry,
this has nothing to do with you—but I'm a ghost and I
prefer to work alone. Why don't you sit down front and
I'll work here. Then at the intermission, with two
perspectives, we can compare notes. I think we'll get
more done that way."

"That's Gareth's goddamn idea, isn't it?" Larry was
screaming, and struggling to rearrange his legs so that he
could stand up. "He wants me out. Out of his show and
out of his life. Well, I'm not going anywhere!"

Someone down front yelled, "Keep it quiet back there!"

Then, contradicting what he'd just said, Larry half
crawled into the aisle, straightened up, and headed toward
the lobby.

No one but me seemed to notice.

Though it briefly crossed my mind to follow him, I
hadn't been hired as a baby-sitter. I picked up my yellow
pad and red pen and went to work.

. . . . .

Almost three hours later, Philip Knight tapped my shoulder. "Lunch break. Sixty minutes." He glanced at my pad filled with notes and the open, edited, messy script in my hand. "Looks as if you've been a busy bee. Would you like to come to Barbetta's with Morgan and me? I'm in an Italian frame of mind."

I'd rather break bread with the devil himself.

"Thanks, but I've made other plans."

"Would you like one of these?" He grinned. "Hot off the press!" He held several *Playbill*s in his left hand. "The printer worked all night. Now all is as it should be—the role of Suzy Q played by Morgan Drake. And, of course, the other cast corrections were made, as well."

I figured the saddest cast correction had to be poor Peggy Malfa, who, instead of moving from Elaine Eden's understudy into the role of Suzy Q, would now be listed as Morgan Drake's understudy.

Knight should take home the Tony in the category Most Arrogant Bastard.

I thumbed through *Playbill*. Great head shot of Morgan. Super lighting. Made her look like a cross between Julia Roberts and Jennifer Lopez. Had I expected anything less?

Though he had top billing, the photograph of Sebastian must have been taken more than a decade ago. Way too wide lapels on his tuxedo and oversized shoulder pads. But decade ago or not, he still looked washed up.

Peggy wasn't a pretty woman, but her narrow face, with those big eyes, small nose, and good skin, had a wholesome quality that belied her apparent heavy drinking. Morgan's second lead ingenue role had gone to her very inexperienced understudy. Why hadn't Philip given that part to Peggy? Because of her drinking? Or because he was a self-centered, mean bastard?

A very handsome bastard. His face would certainly turn on the over-fifty set. A matinee idol look that the dissipated Sebastian James's photo missed by a mile.

I couldn't get over how much Sir Gareth Selby-Steed resembled Miss Piggy. Only missing the wig.

Auturo Como, on the other hand, photographed surprisingly well for a man with three double chins. However, as Mom always said, "It's all in the lighting. A good photographer can make an aardvark attractive."

Cynthia Malone had found a good photographer. Not that she hadn't been—despite Sebastian's cruel comment to Mulroney—very attractive to begin with. I'd thought she'd been quite striking when we first met at the Waldorf. But on this page, with her spiky hair framing her even, if bland, features, and her makeup so perfectly applied, the wardrobe woman looked as if she could be the star.

Larry Cotter's gaunt face radiated despair. Eyes downcast and a scowl in lieu of a smile. But he'd received all the writing credits.

Like the ghost I was, neither my name nor my picture appeared.

Suddenly it occurred to me that the *Suzy Q Playbill* had provided me with the complete lineup of all the suspects. And the cast's and crew's brief biographies had provided me with a game plan.

Nineteen

I was enjoying my second al fresco meal on this otherwise blue Monday, defying my mother's lifelong ban on street vendors. Her mantra: "Where do you think they wash their hands, Jake?"

My hot dog, topped with sauerkraut, relish, and mustard, had been purchased from just such a vendor, along with a bag of potato chips and a Diet Coke. Then, to get in a little exercise, I'd carried my lunch over to Bryant Park, where I now sat on a bench, savoring every bite.

Like much of Manhattan, Bryant Park had undergone a deep cleaning and a face-lift some time ago. Most of the drug addicts, drunks, and other sundry bums had been rousted from its benches. Gradually, mothers and nannies from Tudor City and the high-rises on Second and Third avenues had started to bring the kids here to play, and the office workers, from the Chrysler Building to the Public Library, began to frequent this Midtown oasis, loving the patch of green in the midst of a concrete jungle.

I people-watched. The lady in head-to-toe lavender, singing to a squirrel, would be fodder for some future book.

For dessert, I bought a Good Humor—also from a vendor—but since the ice cream was wrapped and, therefore, not in direct contact with human hands, chocolate malt pops were not included on Maura O'Hara's forbidden foods list.

Feeling far less guilty, I finished my ice cream, licked the stick, and dumped my trash. Then I pulled out a fresh legal pad, reread the *Suzy Q Playbill*, concentrating on the suspects' bios, and made a few notes. Satisfied that I might be onto something, I called the ghosts, reaching Modesty and Jane, and leaving a message for Too Tall Tom, setting up a meeting for tonight at seven. Then I walked west, heading back to work at the Globe.

· · · · ·

Late, naturally, and needing to use the ladies' room, I dashed in the stage door, waving at the guard, who glanced at his watch and frowned. With most of the cast and crew busy, I figured one of the backstage bathrooms should be empty. And what the hell, if the coast was clear, I might be able to do a bit of snooping before I returned to my seat in the last row.

I could hear Morgan Drake's clear soprano onstage. Then Sebastian's whiskey baritone. Good! They were rehearsing their second act duet. I'd use the star's bathroom.

As I dried my hands and checked my makeup, I heard Morgan's dressing room door open, and a woman's voice saying, "I could have killed Elaine Eden."

I froze, blush brush midair. Peggy Malfa! Who was in the room with her?

The understudy sighed deeply, then continued, "God knows I probably had the best motive, though as it turned out, I still wouldn't have been given the Suzy Q role. But don't you see? Even though I had both motive and opportunity to murder Elaine, what earthly reason would I have had for killing her son?"

"But I had a motive, didn't I? Jealousy. You're not suggesting that I killed him, are you?"

Larry Cotter! I wondered what they'd said before entering Morgan's dressing room. And why had they come sneaking in here in the first place? Pretty cheeky, I'd say.

"No," Peggy said, "what I'm saying is that I had good cause to want Elaine Eden dead, and that you, for one, had a heavy-duty reason for removing Tristan Hunter. Eliminating the other man, terrified that you'd lose your knight in tarnished armor to that so-called monk."

"So two separate motives would mean two different killers?" Larry sounded scared.

"Bingo! Of course, Tristan could have discovered who'd killed his mother. Now, that would be a common thread; otherwise, I don't think the deaths are connected."

I literally held my breath. Two killers! Could Peggy's theory have legs? Not good for Too Tall Tom. While he hadn't any reason to kill Eden, I felt certain that Mulroney considered him to be the prime suspect in Tristan Hunter's death.

Larry said, "He could have been blackmailing Elaine's killer."

"I think it's very unlikely that Tristan, at the Baronet for such a short time prior to Elaine's death, had seen or heard anything that would have put his own life in danger." Peggy delivered her lines coldly. "And that brings me back to you, Larry. Have you an alibi for last evening around six? When Mulroney finds out about the Larry-Gareth-Tristan triangle, he'll ask you about your whereabouts, won't he?"

I'd already made sure that the detective knew all about that triangle.

"Christ!" Larry screamed. "Mulroney just called; he's coming to the theater to talk to me later this afternoon."

"Get out of here," Peggy said. "I'm going to search the room."

"Morgan always has it with her."

"Perhaps not onstage, Larry. For God's sake, go have a cigarette or a drink, will you? But you'd damn well better pull yourself together before Homicide arrives. Now go!"

I heard the dressing room door close. Then fast, light steps, as Peggy, seemingly, went speeding around the room. I hopped in the shower, closing the curtain just as she entered the bathroom. I heard drawers being opened, then closed. A rustling sound. Going through papers? Rifling the medicine cabinet? For some reason, maybe answered prayers, Peggy didn't pull back the shower curtain. Her search, which probably had taken less than a minute, seemed an eternity. Suddenly, she was gone. My heart raced and my legs felt like jelly. I don't think I could have stayed still a second longer.

I waited ten minutes, then staggered out of Morgan's dressing room, and into my seat in the last row.

What could Morgan's mysterious item be? And why would Peggy Malfa be risking her career to find it?

Though wardrobe had moved the cast's costumes and props, along with the makeshift set, from the Baronet to the Globe, Morgan's dressing room had seemed rather bare to me.

She, herself, had carried over a large tote, filled with jumbo electric curlers, sundry cosmetics, an electric teakettle, and several boxes of Oreos. A sweatshirt, jeans, and a windbreaker had been thrown over the changing screen. Sneakers tossed in a corner. No doubt those were Morgan's own clothes, the ones that she'd worn to work this morning.

I had no time to dwell on the mini mystery within the mystery. Every fifteen minutes or so, either Philip Knight or Auturo Como would appear at my side, as I made the script changes, alternating in the role of Broadway's highest paid messenger. Then a gofer would run the changes over to Auturo's secretary in the Times Square Building and wait, while she would decipher my rewrites, type the new script's pages, and make copies for the cast and crew.

I've never written so fast before. But rough as it was for me, I knew the actors, especially Morgan—who had to memorize the new lines while they were rehearsing—had it much rougher.

Close to six, as I was putting away my yellow legal pads and red pens, Philip Knight plopped into the seat next to me.

"This has been the most challenging day of my life, Jake." He delivered the line with great drama and a stern demeanor. Then, in an abrupt change of both tone and manner, he said, "Morgan's marvelous, isn't she? I'm convinced our new star will save *Suzy Q!*"

I nodded, then waited, certain that he had something more on his mind.

He waved the last of my changes in the air, and said, "You're doing a super job."

Again I nodded.

"I guess you're working so hard that you haven't had a chance to check out Cynthia." Philip sighed. "Mulroney seems to negate the power of that woman's father figure complex. I'm sure she killed Tristan, too. God knows who's next!"

Could he be trying to convince me that Cynthia Malone had turned into a serial killer, right under our noses?

I decided to try out Peggy Malfa's two killers theory on him. But first I wanted to ask him more about his own theory. "Philip, even if Cynthia is convinced that Sebastian was her biological father, and that Elaine was responsible for her biological mother's suicide, why would she have wanted Tristan dead? He'd have been a kid at the time."

"No doubt he found out that she'd killed his mother. Cynthia had to get rid of him."

"How do you know there aren't two killers on the loose? With two very different motives?"

He blanched, dropped the script pages, and bent,

fumbling to retrieve them. Not quickly enough. I'd seen a fleeting moment of fear distort those handsome features.

Now I tried for a smooth exit line. "Philip, I believe that any one—or two—of the cast or crew could be guilty, and I'd bet Mulroney does, too."

Then, with him still down on his knees, I exited the row via the center aisle.

In the lobby, I grabbed several *Playbill*s, then checked my messages both at home and on my cell phone. Too Tall Tom had left one on the latter, saying he'd see me at seven. Neither Ben nor Dennis had called. I left the theater, thinking you reap what you sow—or however the hell that Biblical quote went.

Twenty

There was a time, not too long ago, when walking at dusk along Ninth Avenue in the middle of Hell's Kitchen would have been considered risky business. God bless our former mayor, he'd made the sidewalks of New York safe. Well, most of them.

Rachel's, one of the relatively new bistros now thriving in these once "mean streets," was on Ninth, between Forty-third and Forty-forth. Though Too Tall Tom was the one who usually discovered restaurants and the rest of us ghosts followed in his wake, I'd stumbled upon Rachel's by accident.

Mom, Gypsy Rose, and I had gone to see *Countess* in a quaint theater on West Forty-fourth, located in a town house, where the audience had to climb two flights of narrow stairs up to the lobby—though management had provided a small elevator for those patrons who couldn't— or wouldn't—navigate the stairs. The intimate, charming theater offered interaction with the players onstage. You could almost reach out and touch them. I felt as if we'd been whisked away to Victorian England and were sitting in the characters' living room.

After having identified so closely with all the adultery angst peculiar to that era, I was starving. We all were. So where could we have dinner at 10:30 P.M.? The Algonquin's Oak Room was an option, but only if we wanted to go into serious long-term credit card debt.

My mother had suggested heading west. "I understand there are several lovely restaurants over on Ninth Avenue." Both Gypsy Rose and I had voiced strong reservations, but Mom persuaded us to forge across Broadway, Seventh, and Eighth. Some of the territory looked pretty daunting, but two cops on horseback, circling the area, and bright streetlights made our journey safe.

As we neared Ninth, I spotted two sites that seemed promising. One even had an outside patio, packed with diners. I'd asked, "How about eating here?"

"No," my mother had said. "Take a left at the corner. I want to consider all of our opportunities."

We'd nixed a grimy diner, filled with grimier people. I suppose if one really wanted to experience the old neighborhood, that might be the place, but we were more interested in exploring the new Ninth Avenue. Then, just before reaching the long-established antiques store on the southeast corner of Ninth and Forty-third, which specialized in Depression pottery and must have been in business since Herbert Hoover's presidency, we passed by Rachel's.

Falling in love with a restaurant is a lot like falling in love with a guy. The sight, the sound, and the smell lure you in. And, when consistently great performance exceeds your expectations, you keep coming back. You bring your friends, to introduce them to your new love. And your relationship is much easier to end. If you find another place that you'd rather frequent, your fickle streak affects only a small part of your former beloved's income, it doesn't break anyone's heart.

As I entered Rachel's, I knew that, as of tonight, I was still in the throes of that passion. And Modesty and Jane were in the throes of yet another argument.

Jane said, "Good. Jake, you can settle this!"

"Can I order a martini first?"

"No! Auturo Como belonged to me! I did all the bloody background grunt work, then, behind my back, Modesty asked Rickie to use his criminal connections to check him out!"

I waved for a waiter.

Rachel's long and narrow interior had a bar on the left as you came in the door, separated from the front tables by a partition. Jane and Modesty had been seated at a table opposite the crowded bar. Pretheater diners filled the back room. The restaurant had lots of loyal customers. Deservedly so. This far west, the lower rent kept the menu prices down, and the eclectic food was delicious.

The bartender acknowledged me, nodded, then raised a shaker, with a questioning look on his rugged face. I nodded back, pleased that I'd become a regular and the bartender knew my favorite cocktail.

Jane did have first dibs on Como; however, I'd be damned no matter what I said, so I took the coward's way out. "Why don't you just tell us what you've learned?" I smiled brightly at Jane, waiting for Modesty to explode.

Instead, she said, "Yeah, go ahead, Jane. We can't sit around here bitching. Too Tall Tom's in trouble. Why the hell should we worry about who had whom?"

Totally amazing! Modesty had mellowed. And, much as I hated to, I had to give the credit to Rickie Romero.

Too Tall Tom arrived, ordered a Cosmopolitan and appetizers for all, and Jane—after a brief discussion of whether she'd prefer to have the mozzarella and tomatoes or the stuffed mushrooms—delivered her report on Auturo Como.

A ghost of Jane's caliber gets around. And New York, in many weird ways, can be a small town. A former client, who'd hired Jane to ghostwrite her memoirs, had grown up on the Lower East Side in the very same tenement as Auturo Como.

Carla Santucci, now around eighty, had made her

money in millinery during the '40s and '50s when all fashionable ladies had topped off their outfits with a hat. She'd started out as a young single woman, working out of the family's cold-water flat, making hats in her bedroom, and using her mother's kitchen table as a desk. Carla had told Jane, "Artie was a punk kid living in the apartment below me. Involved up to his fat butt with the local mob before he turned sixteen."

I asked, "How involved?"

"According to Carla Santucci, Como collected extortion money from the small shop owners. Though 'the enforcer' was as wide as he was high, all that fat must have covered some muscle back then." Jane finished her wine, and ordered another.

Modesty said, "Rickie's informant told him that Como showed no mercy and, eventually, his extortion operation covered the entire Lower East Side."

Jane, not ready to cede center stage, glared at Modesty, and said, "Then Carla's story has just confirmed that. Artie had terrified those store owners, threatening to break their legs on a regular basis. But I gather Rickie's fellow ex-con hasn't been privy to the most important part of Como's story."

"Well, don't make us guess!" Too Tall Tom passed Jane a piece of Italian bread dipped in virgin olive oil.

Jane carefully placed the bread on her plate, and continued, knowing she had everyone's total attention. "Carla Santucci's upstairs neighbor was a Mrs. Buttofuco, who had a granddaughter out in Queens who came back to Granny's kitchen with her mom and dad for pasta and chicken every Sunday. After one of those home-cooked meals, the girl met Auturo Como and they had a hot romance." Jane stared at me and smiled. "You don't have to guess the girl's name, do you, Jake."

I said, "Maria Elena Buttofuco!"

Modesty asked, "And just who the hell is that?"

"Elaine Eden," Jane said, sounding so smug that I

wouldn't have blamed Modesty for breaking both her legs.

But Modesty attempted a sweeter revenge. "Well, what makes you think that's so important? Auturo himself told Jake that he'd had an affair with Elaine. From what he said, apparently, he dumped her because she'd put on weight. Since he's the size of Rhode Island, isn't that a hoot? Maybe Elaine actually dumped him."

"That's just the point, Modesty," Jane said, "no one dumped anyone. Maria Elena's father was Auturo's counterpart in Queens. Part of the same crime family. Rumor had it that her father had fixed the Miss Rheingold contest."

Jesus, wait till my mother heard that!

"Elaine and Auturo's bond lasted through all her marriages and divorces. And through all their very public scenes. The producer and the star seemed to need each other." Jane shook her head. "Some sort of sick codependance. They'd fight, say terrible things publicly, then make up. They carried on like that for over fifty years. Carla Santucci, who stayed in touch with both of them over all those years, swears that Elaine's only true love was Auturo Como."

I said, "And Auturo had been convinced that Tristan killed his mother. Damn! Maybe Como turned around and killed Hunter in order to avenge Elaine's death."

Too Tall Tom sighed, then wiped his eyes with a napkin. "Tell that to Lt. Mulroney."

Modesty flicked a wrist in Too Tall Tom's direction. "For God's sake, if you killed every guy who broke your heart, you'd be a mass murderer! Even a homicide cop's smart enough to figure that out."

"That's unkind, Modesty," he said, "and unfair. I had strong feelings for Tristan Hunter and, even though the man disappointed me, I'm totally crushed by his death!"

"Yeah," Modesty said, "well, we have to move along here. I have a report of my own to give."

Knowing that she'd really been worried about Too Tall

Tom before he arrived at Rachel's, I figured this had to be the Modesty Meade interpretation of tough love.

I patted his arm, then turned to her. "Go ahead, Modesty, we're waiting."

"Cynthia Malone and I had tea at Sarabeth's this afternoon. That's why I'm not too hungry, but I came to this dinner anyway because I want to solve these murders before your mother's wedding, so we ghosts can have a good time!"

Modesty's way of saying: Don't worry, Too Tall Tom, you'll be off the hook with Homicide by Friday. A small grin had brightened his face as she spoke.

"Did you learn anything new?" After all these years, her scowl still scares me. "Sorry, of course, I'm sure you did!"

"I went there with a specific goal in mind." Modesty nodded sagely in my direction. "And, as you all know, I achieve my goals."

Well, except for her edited, but still unfinished, mammoth Gothic novel. Modesty might never complete that goal in this lifetime. However, since she claims to be descended from vampires, that might not a problem.

Jane snarled, "Are you going to sit there and gloat over your detective work or are you going to reveal its results? Some of us are hungry, even if you aren't, and I want to order."

"Shut up, Jane," Modesty said, "you had your turn and, as I'm sure we all agree, a rather disappointing one. Not a Perry Mason moment."

"Please!" A head at the bar spun in my direction. I lowered my voice. "Go on, Modesty, what was your goal? And what did Cynthia tell you?"

"I wanted to find out why Morgan Drake had shown up at rehearsal on the day that Elaine was murdered, wearing that red jumpsuit!"

Jeez! Score one for Modesty. The jumpsuit had piqued my curiosity, too. But with all that had gone on since

Saturday, I'd almost forgotten about it. I gave her a high five.

She continued, sounding very Nancy Drew-ish. "And who better to ask than the wardrobe mistress?"

Too Tall Tom said, "Great work, Modesty! What did this Malone woman say?"

"That Elaine's understudy, Peggy Malfa, arrived drunk on Saturday morning—not for the first time—and Philip Knight sent her home to sleep it off. Then he ordered Cynthia to alter one of Elaine's extra jumpsuits to fit Morgan Drake. As Cynthia took in the costume, she overheard Philip tell Morgan that on opening night, she would be starring as Suzy Q."

I said, "How could Knight have known that unless he'd planned on eliminating Elaine?"

Modesty looked pleased. "Right! And Cynthia said that's exactly the same question that Lt. Mulroney had asked her when she told him about the jumpsuit!"

Twenty-one

I decided to wait for dessert to dish out my *Playbill* theory. No sense ruining everyone's entrée. Besides, Too Tall Tom needed to talk about his relationship with Tristan, then grieve a bit; Modesty, our bride-to-be, should get a chance to chat about the two upcoming weddings; and Jane's most recent adventure in Bloomingdale's had yet to be explored.

"This is delicious, Jake. Would you like a taste?" With so much of him to fill, Too Tall Tom, as usual, had ordered two main courses. He was offering me a slice of his duck.

"No, thanks, you know I never eat anything *fowler* than a chicken. But you can put a little of that shrimp and angel hair pasta on my bread plate."

Jane said, "Really dreadful joke, Jake."

Too Tall Tom complied with my request, but frowned less than graciously as he served me one teeny-weeny shrimp and a minuscule portion of his pasta.

Modesty caught my eye and winked. "I'll have some shrimp, too. Does it taste as good as it looks?"

Too Tall Tom sighed. "Try the duck, Modesty."

"You know what you can do with that duck . . ."

Jane reached over and speared a shrimp off Too Tall Tom's plate. "Grief doesn't seem to have curbed your appetite."

"Contrary to what you three witches seem to believe, I'm actually very sad. Tristan Hunter's reappearance brought a candle into a room with no light. He arrived at a time when I had no one and my life had little meaning. His glow warmed my heart."

"What happened to that cabdriver?" Jane took another shrimp.

Too Tall Tom slapped her wrist. "If you would stop shopping long enough to call your friends once in a while, you'd know that he married a transsexual to get his green card."

"Go on," I said, "old loves can make us crazy." I shut up, thinking of Dennis, then felt flushed and flustered, wondering if the ghosts realized that I was thinking about Dennis.

"I allowed him to use me again. Same old selfish Tristan . . . same old gullible me!" Too Tall Tom pushed both of his plates away. This was serious! "You'd think that, after all those years as a monk, the man might have developed a smidgen of morality."

Modesty said, "If you're not going to finish that shrimp, can I have the rest of it?"

Only if she shared it with me.

Too Tall Tom ignored her. "So now the police believe I murdered my former lover. And, the truth is, I could have killed him." He chuckled nervously. "If someone hadn't gotten to him first."

Since Jane, Modesty, and I knew that Too Tall Tom was no Terminator, we divided his pasta and shrimp three ways, and moved on.

Jane and I ordered café au lait, but passed on dessert. Too Tall Tom—who seemed to have made a quick recovery—and Modesty opted for a cinnamon and orange concoction that they planned on sharing, and double espressos. God, they'd be up all night. Of course, Modesty, who claimed to be a direct descendent of Count Dracula, liked to prowl around till three or four in the morning and, in Rickie, she'd found a kindred cat, but Too Tall Tom would be tossing and turning till dawn.

If they were going to be sleep-deprived, they might as well be working on the case. I pulled the *Suzy Q Playbill*s out of my briefcase and gave one to each of the ghosts. "Hot off the presses. Dedicated to Elaine Eden, but otherwise, the show's former star is merely a rapidly fading memory. No tributes. Not even a photograph. She's dead and she's history."

Jane picked up a *Playbill* and flipped through it. "In addition to her head shot and bio, Morgan Drake's face keeps popping up."

"Doesn't it?" I nodded. "Speaking of bios, notice how short, sweet, and vague Morgan's is. Nary a word about her past. Nothing about where she was born, where she grew up, or if she has any family."

Modesty, reading over Jane's shoulder, said, "Yeah. That is odd. These days, most cast and crew biographies gush on and on, thanking dear old Mom and Dad, sundry aunties, drama coaches, agents, past and current lovers, and the first person to give them an orgasm. But Morgan's is so impersonal, it's cold."

"Read Cynthia Malone's and Peggy Malfa's," I said, "both of them, like Morgan, seemed to have arrived on this earth in their late twenties. No parents noted with gratitude, no childhood success stories, no significant other. No past."

Too Tall Tom shook his head. "But, Jake, they're not the show's stars. Wardrobe mistresses and understudies usually don't get many lines."

I pointed to the open page in Jane's *Playbill*. Sebastian's dresser had thanked no less than six people, and the assistant to the lighting director had more copy than Cynthia, Peggy, and Morgan combined. "They do in this *Playbill*."

Jane said, "Jake's right. Why are these women avoiding their pasts?"

"Good question," I said, "and I'm convinced that the motive for these two murders will be found in the killer's past. Look at the history of crossed paths in this case. Elaine and Tristan, mother and son, both murdered. Auturo and Elaine, longtime lovers. Elaine and Sebastian, married and divorced three times. Philip and Auturo, business partners. Philip and Elaine, engaged to be married. Philip and Morgan, having an affair. Cynthia's story about being Sebastian's daughter. Peggy and Larry, drinking buddies, digging for dirt in Morgan's dressing room. Larry and Gareth. Gareth and Tristan. Larry and Tristan."

Too Tall Tom groaned. "Don't forget about Tristan and me. That star-crossed past is Lt. Mulroney's favorite intersection."

"Okay," I said, "your assignments, if you choose to accept them, are . . ."

Modesty said, "To check out these characters' pasts, see how their lives intertwined, and figure out which one of them had the motive, means, and opportunity to murder Elaine and Tristan."

Like the angels they really were, the ghosts accepted the assignment.

. . . . .

An hour later, back in Carnegie Hill, I thought, this has been one hell of a long day.

I heard Mom and Gypsy Rose giggling as I opened the front door. They were playing Scrabble. Apparently, my mother had just used her tiles to make one of George Carlin's seven words that can't be said on television. Or, at least, couldn't have been said back in the '70s. With the wedding now only a few days away, this might be Mom's last board game as a single woman.

I laughed. "You won't find that dirty word in the official Scrabble dictionary, Mrs. O'Hara!"

"Jake, you scared me," my mother said, "but I'm glad

you're home. Did you have a nice dinner with the ghosts?"

"Great," I said. "We should all go down to Rachel's sometime, soon!"

When? Mom would be a Washington wife. And I'd be eating on my own most of the time. I gave each of them a kiss on the cheek. "I have some more rewrites to do, so I'll see you ladies tomorrow."

"A nice cup of tea?" My mother sounded guilty, as well she should.

What the hell was the matter with me? I guess knowing you're acting crazy doesn't stop you from feeling crazy. Intellectually, I was happy for my mother. Emotionally, like a child, I somehow resented her getting married and leaving me all alone in our Carnegie Hill co-op.

"Okay, Mom. But make sure it's decaf."

When she went into the kitchen, I slumped into a chair next to Gypsy Rose.

"Wedding day blues, Jake?"

I looked into her warm, caring face, and felt a tear start down my own. "I don't know, Gypsy Rose. Maybe I'm just tired."

"Your father is worried about you."

I had no doubt about that.

She took my hand in hers. "Zelda wants to talk to you, Jake. She seems edgy and, with all due respect, sounded more than a little demanding. I'll be channeling James Hilton, too. Invite the ghosts, especially Too Tall Tom. I think Tristan Hunter may have a message for him. Tomorrow night, my house, at seven. Okay?"

The concern in her voice alarmed me. I knew she believed every word that she said, and I also knew how much she loved me. "I'll call them as soon as I finish my tea. What about Mom? Will she and Aaron be there?"

"No. This séance sounds like serious business, and I don't want to upset Maura so close to the wedding . . ."

"Here we go!" My mother, carrying a tray, came back

into the room. "There's nothing like a nice cup of tea to make you feel better."

. . . . .

I confirmed the channeling with Too Tall Tom and Modesty, and left Jane a message. Then checked my own. Neither Dennis nor Ben had called.

Twenty-two

Standing on the Fifth Avenue bus Tuesday morning, as we were stuck in traffic at Fifty-ninth Street for a full ten minutes, I decided that I should have taken the subway. But on such a glorious autumn morning, with the air so sweet and the sky so clear, I wanted to walk from Fifth Avenue over to the Globe. Now I'd never make it to the theater on time.

Tomorrow, Lt. Mulroney would allow the entire cast and crew to return to the Baronet to rehearse, with all the costumes and the much missed scenery and larger props.

No pre-opening previews for this show. We'd rehearse on Wednesday morning and have a dress rehearsal that night before opening on Thursday. And I still hadn't finished the rewrites for act three!

Ordinarily, I try to write when stuck in traffic; however, standing, with a teenager's backpack abutting my shoulder blades and a fat guy's briefcase in close contact with my kneecaps, I had neither the mobility nor the motivation to pull out pen and pad. So I gripped my pole, shared with several other sweaty hands, closed my eyes, and conjured up Morgan Drake's dressing room.

What had Peggy Malfa been searching for? Something small enough to hide in a drawer or cabinet. Larry had said that Morgan usually kept *it* with her. Something small enough to tote around then. A notebook or journal that she kept in a purse? Surely Morgan wouldn't carry her purse onstage. Maybe something that she wore every day. So commonplace that no one would notice. Like a piece of jewelry? A watch? A ring? Or a medal hidden under her clothing? But why would Peggy believe that a piece of Morgan's jewelry—or whatever—had been connected to the murders?

We started moving again, the driver inching downtown at the snail's pace New Yorkers accepted as norm.

I'd have a chat with Peggy. My mind also moved on. To Cynthia Malone.

If Morgan, as Larry's suggestion had led me to believe, kept *it* on her person at all times, Cynthia, her dresser, might know what *it* was, without even knowing she knew.

The longer we remained tied up in traffic, the more convoluted my thought processes became.

I quickly decided to invite Cynthia for lunch at Barrymore's and to stop thinking till I got off the bus.

Unfortunately, as soon as I put the case on hold, my mind became flooded with images of Dennis and Ben. Should I call the former and explain why I'd kissed the latter? Did I know why? And, if Dennis hadn't called because he'd been jealous, peeved, or disappointed, what was Ben's excuse? Had that been a kiss-off kiss? I hadn't thought so Sunday night. But maybe this was Ben's belated payback for my jaunt last summer to Venice with Dennis. Had I managed to totally screw things up with both of them? I really missed—

"Lady, would you move over and let me by?" The fat man poked my thigh with the metal tip of his briefcase. "I want to get off and you're blocking the aisle!"

My God! We were at Forty-second Street. I'd mused right by my stop.

I glared at the fat man, shoving his briefcase away from

my leg, then stepping forward, halting his progress, as I headed for the front door. "Just a minute, mister! Don't you know women and children are the first ones off the bus?"

· · · · ·

Larry Cotter crouched in the last row, staring straight ahead to the empty stage, looking glum and uncomfortable, and holding neither pen nor paper in his clutched hand.

The orchestra, now squeezed into a much smaller pit than the Baronet's, was playing the next to last melody of the overture. Sir Gareth Selby-Steed's music soared. Dramatic. Triumphant. Loud.

I hadn't missed much after all.

"Morning, Larry."

He jumped, obviously startled and, seemingly, as far from reality as I'd been on the bus.

"Our ghost, the writer with no name, but all the acclaim, has stolen the scene." He'd slurred through the entire sentence.

I glanced at my watch. Nine-thirty. And Larry Cotter was, as Zelda Fitzgerald would have said, three sheets to the wind. Feeling no pain. Blotto. Smashed. Flying. High as a kite.

I heard Auturo Como's bellow before I saw him come charging up the aisle. "Cotter, I told you to go home. You're fired. I want you out of here! Now!"

Larry unscrambled those extraordinarily long legs and stood up, wobbling, but steadying himself on the back of the chair in the row in front of us. "And I told you, you fat, ugly American pig, no one fires me but Gareth. We come as a package." Then he burst into song. *"You can't have one without the other!"*

I regretted getting off the bus.

Auturo turned scarlet. He sputtered, but no words came out. The producer looked like a man about to have a stroke.

"Auturo, are you okay?" I reached for his hand, trying to take his pulse. He yanked it away from me.

Philip Knight and Gareth Selby-Steed, approaching from opposite directions, arrived at the same time.

While Knight fussed over his partner, Sir Selby-Steed turned his wrath on his. "You're finished, Larry. Finished with *Suzy Q* and finished with me. You're a bloody no-talent drunk. Your trite words have mucked up my music for the first and the last time. And God only knows what other evil your insane jealousy has spawned." Gareth's voice rose. Shrill. Vicious. "Get out of this theater and out of my life!"

Sir Selby-Steed's hyperbole struck me as being even more trite than Larry's libretto, but not wanting to continue working next to a drunk, I reserved judgment. Would this Broadway horror show ever end? I couldn't wait till opening night.

After a surprisingly docile Cotter had gone, the unholy trinity, Como, Knight, and Selby-Steed, sweet-talked me over the sound of increasingly louder music. Then, mercifully, the overture ended, the curtain rose, and I went to work.

At the lunch break, I caught up with Cynthia Malone backstage. Juggling an armful of costumes, she was attempting to open the door to Morgan Drake's dressing room.

"Hi, Cynthia."

"Oh, Jake, how you doing? Did you hear what happened to Larry?"

I held the door open, then followed her into the room. "Yes. I found myself in the middle of his termination."

"How could Selby-Steed be so cruel? Larry adores him, don't you know? Why, I believe that he would kill for Gareth." She stopped short, then tittered nervously. "Well, that's just a manner of speaking, isn't it?"

"Look, Cynthia, if you're free, I'd like to take you to lunch. Barrymore's?" I remembered how much I'd liked her the first time we'd met.

"That would be jolly, wouldn't it?" She laid the clothes on the bed, then grabbed some hangers from the rack. "But I always go home for lunch to see my babies."

"I didn't know you had children."

"Caesar and Cleopatra. They're named for Sebastian James's biggest success in West End. And though I do think of them as children, actually, they're Siamese cats. But don't ever tell them that."

I laughed. "I'd like to see them."

"Oh. Are you a cat person, Jake?"

"I am." Not really a lie. Since I'd never taken any position, pro or con, I could be considered a cat person.

"Well, come home with me. I live on West Twenty-ninth. Between Eighth and Ninth. I usually walk, and it's such a lovely day." She was placing the costumes on the clothes rack in the order that Morgan would be wearing them. "Let me finsh up here, and I'll meet you at the stage door in five minutes."

Smiling, I said, "Perfect!"

. . . . .

"Jake O'Hara, right? We met the other day in Sardi's."

Waiting at the stage door, wondering where the guard had disappeared to, I spun around and, at first, thought that Morgan Drake had spoken to me. In full Suzy Q makeup and costume, the plain Peggy Malfa looked uncannily like the glamorous star.

"Thought I was Morgan, didn't you?" Peggy sounded amused.

I nodded.

"An amazing transformation, isn't it? Cynthia Malone is damn good at her job."

"Yes, so I see." I felt uncomfortable. Not sure how to handle this. I couldn't very well say, Gee Peggy, you're so much more attractive as Morgan. And, though smiling, she seemed distracted. Maybe Peggy would rather look like herself.

As if reading my mind, she laughed, and said, "I'll be myself again at six. That washed, scrubbed, simple, down-to-earth gal that no one knows or loves. Can you meet me for a drink then, Jake? At Barrymore's? I need to talk to you."

"Perfect!" I said, for the second time in less than five minutes.

Twenty-three

An **afternoon chill** had settled in and a light wind accompanied it. Feeling glad that I'd worn my camel hair blazer and a turtleneck sweater, I increased my pace. Cynthia Malone had long legs and moved with a fast stride. We walked the fifteen blocks in as many minutes.

Our destination turned out to be a shabby town house, a walk-up, in a west Chelsea neighborhood, on the cusp of becoming trendy.

"I live on the fourth floor," she said, "but the exercise keeps me in shape."

The railroad flat's three rooms and bath had been infused with massive doses of Cynthia's unique style. For a woman who dressed in head-to-toe black, she'd decorated the entire apartment in primary colors.

We entered a kitchen, equipped with what appeared to be the original stove. The wallpaper was a maze of yellow jonquils, and the wooden floorboards had been painted in the same shade as the flowers. She'd found an antique table, painted it with white enamel, topped it with yellow place mats, and surrounded it with four white high-back chairs. Two big baskets, lined in yellow quilted fabric, stood in one corner.

"Do the cats sleep in those?"

As I asked, the two Siamese in question, sporting matching yellow ribbons, sauntered into the room.

"Only when catnapping. At night, they sleep with me." Cynthia bent to stroke her pets, who were staring suspiciously at me. "Come, I'll show you the rest of the place."

The living room, plush red velvet and gold fringe—*The Best Little Whorehouse in Texas* came to mind—turned out to be a shrine to Sebastian James. Posters of his plays, publicity photos spanning decades, and candid shots taken over many years, probably without the subject ever being aware, hung on all four walls.

Cynthia smiled, then swept her arm out in a grand gesture. "Isn't it wonderful?"

"Something to behold," I said.

One of the three dark mahogany tables, all covered in that damn fringed velvet, held a large picture of an English country cottage, nestled among rolling hills, where a sweet little girl and a lovely young woman were frolicking on the front lawn. A slim man, his head turned away from the camera, stood behind them. I picked the photograph up. "What a beautiful child!" I spoke only the truth.

"Thank you! That's me, with my real mother and father. I'm adopted, you know, raised here in the States, but I was born in Britain."

I wondered if she'd tell me that Sebastian James was her biological father, but a long moment passed, and she remained silent.

I gave her a weak smile, clueless about what to say next, and starting to feel on edge. This shrine seemed so sick. So sad. Cynthia could be certifiable. Could she also be a killer?

"Come into the kitchen, I have a lovely tuna salad all ready to eat."

While she served lunch, I quickly changed the subject from Sebastian to Morgan.

"My mother and I have a hobby—we collect theater trivia, with a special interest in the stars' superstitions." I'd played a wild card and, if my gamble proved to be the wrong move, I might never learn what Peggy and Larry had been searching for! "I've heard that Morgan Drake always wears a keepsake—maybe her very own lucky charm—something that she never removes. Even onstage. Is that true?"

Cynthia blinked, then leaned in close to me. "So you've heard about the locket?" She emphasized the word *locket*, making it sound like a conspiracy.

My turn to remain silent.

"Then you know Morgan hadn't always worn that locket. I saw it for the first time about three weeks ago. I don't believe she ever owned a locket prior to that time, though she claims it had belonged to her maternal grandmother. But you're certainly right about her never taking it off."

"What does it look like? Is it unusual in any way? A valuable antique? Do you think it has any special significance, other than being a Drake family heirloom?"

"I want you to understand that you're questioning a prejudiced party here. Not for all the tea in China would I ever believe that locket had been passed down from dear old Granny. Especially since I'm convinced that Morgan herself sprang from the loins of a jackal. But Jake, it's a very ordinary locket, so commonplace, that no one can prove otherwise."

"Prove otherwise?" Cynthia had me totally confused.

"Righto." She rattled her cup, then placed it on the yellow place mat. "Just a run-of-the-mill gold locket. Circa 1930, I'd say. Though they were very similar, almost identical, there was no way to prove Morgan's locket was the same one that Peggy Malfa had lost."

"What?"

"Yes. Peggy's locket had gone missing the very week

before Morgan started wearing her *'family heirloom.'*"

Beyond bizarre.

"And you say the two lockets were similar?"

"Identical, except for the *M* engraved on the front of Morgan's. But, of course, she could have gone to any jewelry store in New York City to have that *M* engraved on Peggy's locket, now couldn't she?"

I took a bite of the tuna salad. Excellent. "This is great, Cynthia. Thanks for inviting me."

"My pleasure. I can tell the cats like you. You can come visit us anytime. Now, is that all you need to know about the locket?"

"One more thing: Had you ever actually seen Peggy's locket before she misplaced it?"

Cynthia eyes opened wide. "Not that I can recall. Why, is that important?"

"Well, someone must have seen it, right? Someone who could confirm that the locket had been in Peggy's possession before Morgan started wearing it, and that there had been no *M* engraved on it then."

"Larry," she said immediately, "he and Peggy are good mates. He'd be able to back up her story. Not that I think it needs confirmation, Jake. No one connected with *Suzy Q* trusts Morgan."

Mates. Blimey! Cynthia's use of English slang had to be an affectation. British born or not, no child raised in the USA would refer to close friends as good mates.

· · · · ·

During our walk back to the Globe, I remembered to ask about another piece of the puzzle. "Cynthia, that first day I came to the Baronet, you threw out a really funny line."

"I did?"

"Yes. When Elaine complained that her red jumpsuit was too tight, you had a great comeback. Something about her late-night bourbon and bonbon binge."

She smiled. "I actually made the audience laugh, didn't

I? That sort of heady stuff doesn't happen to me very often."

"You'd been with her late Friday after she and Philip Knight had left Barrymore's? I know that Elaine and Sebastian had staged quite a scene at the restaurant, and that you'd gotten Sebastian cleaned up and out of there. So, where and when did you witness Elaine's bourbon and bonbon binge?"

Cynthia stopped smiling. She stopped walking, too, and put her hands on her hips. "Who do you think you are, Jake, Lt. Mulroney? I may have to answer his questions, but I sure as hell don't have to answer yours! And when I tell Caesar and Cleopatra about your boorish behavior, you'll never be welcome in our home again!"

Twenty-four

Other than the gofers, who'd picked up my rewrites as soon as I made them and whisked them away, I worked straight through from 2:00 to 5:30, with no other human contact.

Then I hustled over to Barrymore's, hoping Peggy Malfa would show up on time. I had a séance at seven. But I also had an insatiable curiosity.

The place was packed. Not a seat at the bar. Nor an empty table. The lower prices on the 5:00-to-7:00 pre-theater dinners had attracted a large flock of early birds. Tourists in windbreakers and baseball caps. New Yorkers in basic black. More leather than wool. Editors from the nearby publishing houses and law firms, meeting friends. And there were several actors in casual, almost sloppy, attire, doing some serious drinking at the bar.

I squeezed in between a handsome Texan wearing a Stetson and a smile, and a morose, boozy, craggy-faced character actor, whom I recognized from his recent role as a killer on a *Law & Order* episode. I asked the bartender for a white wine spritzer, but he and his partner were so damn busy, my drink probably wouldn't arrive till after I was long gone.

Just as the Texan leaned down to talk to me, my cell phone rang.

"Save my spot," I said, smiling up at him. "I'll be back."

Times Square rocked round the clock. At six in the evening, it absolutely exploded. I shouted, "Hello!"

"Jake?"

Ben! My heart beat louder than the thundering herds of humanity bearing down on me. These crossroads of New York have to be the most traveled path in the world.

"Yes . . ."

"I can hardly hear you, Jake."

"I'm standing on the corner of Forty-fifth and Eighth, so speak up." Good. Maybe he hadn't heard the quaver in my voice.

"Look, I'm on my way to a crime scene, but I think you should know that Elaine Eden's autopsy revealed an extremely high dosage of tranquilizers in her blood. That explains why she never noticed the rope had been sliced. Mulroney has just picked up Philip Knight and is bringing him to Midtown North for questioning."

"Why? I mean why Philip?"

"His motive might have been to have his mistress star as Suzy Q. Maybe that's too obvious. But since Philip and Elaine lived together, he had the best shot of tampering with her pills. And, though she frequently threatened to reduce her philandering fiancé to a codicil, it turns out that Philip not only inherited Elaine's entire stock portfolio, he also got the beach house in the Hamptons, worth millions."

"Really? What about Tristan? Didn't Elaine leave anything to her son?"

"Not much. Her Tony Awards and her Oscar. Family photographs. Stuff like that. No cash or property."

"What a witch!"

"Right. Anyway, Mulroney checked out Knight's

phone records. He'd called Tristan at the Leo House on Sunday, prior to Sebastian's threatening call. Mulroney thinks Tristan may have stumbled onto something linking Philip to Elaine's death. And that Philip may have brought the Oscar along to use as a weapon."

"But that makes no sense. Too Tall Tom told us that Tristan had been afraid of Sebastian James, not Philip Knight."

"Tristan might not have realized that Knight posed a danger." Was Ben being testy? Or did his raised voice only make him seem so? "Mulroney believes Tristan must have been blackmaing Philip"

"Yeah, maybe," I said, but I didn't buy it.

"Well, Nancy Drew, it looks as if this case may be closed. Go home, relax, have some fun with Maura and Aaron. I'll be seeing you."

I never got to say good-bye. But before he hung up, I heard him say, "Sandy, I'll be right with you!"

Ben Rubin had dashed off to investigate a different crime with his partner in Homicide, the tall, slender, brunette Sandy Ellis, the sexiest, best dressed, longest-legged detective in the Nineteenth Precinct. Hell, in all of the city.

Despite reacting to Ben's aside in a manner that might be considered jealously, the man on my mind was Dennis. I desperately wanted to speak to him. Had kissing Ben screwed up my relationship with Dennis forever?

I went back to the bar.

Peggy Malfa, minus makeup and wearing jeans and a tweed jacket, stood next to the tall Texan, drinking what had to be my white wine.

"Hi, Peggy," I said.

"Little lady, I thought you deserted me," Tex drawled.

I spotted two stools at the far end of the bar and gestured in their direction. "Come on, Peggy, let's move back there."

"Are you all going to abandon me?"

"We vant to be alone," I said, doing a very poor Garbo,

while placing a ten-dollar bill on the bar. "Sorry, cow-boy."

Peggy carried the wineglass with her.

I glanced at my watch as we took our seats. "I have less than ten minutes, Peggy. What did you want to talk to me about?"

"An associate of yours, a Ms. Jane Dowling, showed up at the Globe early this morning, laying in wait for me. Said she was a freelance writer, wanting to profile an understudy, so I agreed to let her interview me during the lunch break. Is it true that you sent this woman to see me?"

"Yes. Jane's a fine freelance writer, and two of her profiles have been published in *New York* magazine." I didn't add that each of them had run under someone else's byline.

"She turned out to be a nosy bitch. I suspected as much this morning and I should never have agreed to talk to her." Peggy waved to the bartender, who, surprisingly, came over at once. "I'll have a double Dewar's on the rocks."

He turned to me. "What would you like?"

"Nothing, thanks. I'm leaving."

When he left to get her drink, Peggy continued her tirade. "Tell your friend that my past belongs only to me. That I never discuss my parents. Or how I was raised. And that I'll sue her skinny designer-covered butt, if she prints one goddamn word of that garbage she claims to have unearthed."

What in God's name had Jane dug up?

Twenty-five

"Zelda's here, where the hell have you been? The séance started without you!" Jane stood at the bottom of the old circular staircase that led from Gypsy Rose's New Age street level bookstore up to her residence.

Browsers were roaming the aisles, scanning titles, and perusing pages. The long, chatty checkout line went clear back to the tea shop, where every table was filled with readers enjoying lattes and literature.

"Sorry."

She glared at me. "Sorry doesn't cut it, Jake. We assembled at your request. Even the dead showed up on schedule! And Zelda's been asking for you. Your time management skills stink!" Jane waved in the direction of the well-stocked shelves. "Pick up one of my ghosted self-help books before you leave here tonight. Start with *Time Control for Slow Learners*!"

As if Jane wasn't always late. Or sneaking off shopping. I wanted to lash out, but she had a point. Damn it! Once again my curiosity had gotten me into trouble. I'd offended Zelda Fitzgerald and Gypsy Rose Liebowitz. Two of my favorite people.

As we quickly climbed the Persian carpeted steps, Jane said, "Of course, Zelda arrived somewhat unexpectedly, before the channeling began. Gypsy Rose wanted to wait till you arrived. But I guess the world beyond waits for no mere mortal. Not even Jake O'Hara."

I tightened my grip on the old oak banister. I could strangle her. Surely a jury would consider it justifiable homicide.

Oblivious to my thoughts of murder, she looked back in anger. "Zelda brought James Hilton along with her. I think they have new information about Tristan. You really are the most inconsiderate . . ."

We'd reached Gypsy Rose's office on the third floor. Jane opened the door.

The chandelier cast a warm glow. Gypsy Rose sat in the big burgundy leather chair behind her mission-period desk in the center of the lovely room. Her eyes sparkled, her mouth formed an almost perfect circle, the fingers of her left hand ran playfully through her hair. No question about it—that is, if one actually believed in this world beyond theory—Gypsy Rose was gone; Zelda was in residence.

Modesty and Too Tall Tom were seated on one of a matching pair of gray tweed love seats. I perched on its mate, directly across the small room from them. Jane sat down beside me.

I noticed Dennis, standing motionless, off to the left of Gypsy Rose's desk, in front of the velvet drapes. The psychic as matchmaker?

"Jake! Is that you?" Zelda sounded very Southern tonight and possibly a tad tipsy.

"Yes. Sorry I'm late."

I felt Dennis's eyes on me and glanced in his direction. He cocked his head and winked. Flustered, I felt a shiver of desire travel from my tongue to my toes. I winked back.

"You're forgiven. Scott always said I'd be late for my own funeral." I heard Jane start a sigh, then stifle it. Zelda continued, "Now, before we get down to murder, I have a message from your father."

"What did he say?"

While I seriously questioned, despite some strong evidence to the contrary, much of Gypsy Rose's psychic connections, I still hungered to accept even the most remote possibility that I could be in some sort of communication with my dead father.

"Well, sugar, I hope you understand this message, because I sure don't. Jack wants you to look in his mother's old steamer trunk. He says you know where it's stored. And when you open it, you'll find the solution to your biggest problem." Zelda rolled Gypsy Rose's eyes. "What might that problem be, Jake?"

I stared down at my shoes and lied. "I don't know."

The lilt of her laughter filled the tiny room. "Then I suggest you open that trunk and find out!"

"I will."

"Good! Now James Hilton wants to talk to all of you. But before I skedaddle, I want you to consider a ghost-writing job, Jake."

"Oh?" I felt puzzled. "For whom?" Zelda has been Gypsy Rose's longtime spirit guide, and I never expected that she might be in contact with any living people other than our crowd.

"For me, silly. The muse has returned. Obviously, *Save Me the Waltz* didn't get all the writing out of my system."

This time Jane uttered a sigh heard around the room. Modesty screamed, "Wow!" Too Tall Tom clapped.

I sputtered, "You?"

"Jake," Zelda said, "I do trust that your writing ability far exceeds your comprehension skill."

I wondered.

"I've outlined a jazz age murder mystery, starring me as the protagonist. I've always been a great detective. Scott will be my Watson. Ernest, Maxwell, and the Murphys will be among the prime suspects And you, my dear, will be the ghost."

"But—"

"Jake, we'll discuss this matter at another time. I'm off. Here's James!"

Gypsy Rose went slack, her mouth agape. Then she sat up straight, no longer Zelda. James Hilton said, "I have a message from Tristan."

Too Tall Tom jumped up and moved closer to the desk. "Who killed him?"

James Hilton, using Gypsy Rose's voice, said, "I'm terribly sorry, I can't answer your question. Although Tristan indicated that the answer can be found in the past. As he has told you—it's all in the family—however, he cannot be more specific than that." The voice might be Gypsy Rose's but the phraseology and the delivery sure as hell weren't.

"Why didn't he come here himself?" Too Tall Tom demanded, then looked abashed, as if he'd realized that he was questioning one ghost about another ghost's whereabouts.

James Hilton said, "Tristan feels very guilty about all that greed and lust cropping up just before he died. So his soul is now in a place devoted primarily to prayer and repentance. A peaceful plane. I often visit there myself. Reminds me of *Lost Horizon*."

Before Too Tall Tom really got in Hilton's face—well, actually, in Gypsy Rose's—I jumped in. "Please, Mr. Hilton, did Tristan say anything else?"

"Only that he certainly had not been blackmailing anyone."

Then why had he been murdered? The two-killer concept flashed back into my mind. I'd bet that Elaine Eden's Oscar had been in her son's possession. Tristan's killer could have struck on impulse and simply reached for the nearest heavy object.

Too Tall Tom couldn't remain silent. "Mr. Hilton, did Tristan ask you to tell me anything?"

Gypsy Rose's head nodded, and James Hilton said, "Yes, he did. He said, 'Tell Too Tall Tom that I'm sorry

I behaved so shabbily toward him. I promise to do better the next time around.' You see, he believes that the two of you are fated to be together in a future incarnation."

Dennis Kim spoke for the first time. "Hey, Jake, maybe that's our destiny, too. We've just been suffering from the wrong karma this time around."

Twenty-six

Gypsy Rose, herself again, bustled around her kitchen, getting ready to serve us dinner. With the table already set, a fire lit, and the beef stew simmering, sending up an aroma that no one could resist, we'd all accepted her invitation.

Aaron and Mom were at Gracie Mansion tonight. Some bipartisan political thing. Cocktails, followed by dinner at the Four Seasons with the mayor and several members of the city council. I suspected my mother would thrive in that environment, considering it a dress rehearsal for her new role as a Washington wife. As usual my emotions were mixed, glad for Mom, but sorry for myself. I damn well better snap out of this.

I passed on a martini, wanting a clear head. As soon as I arrived home, I planned on going down to our storage room in the basement and prying open my paternal grandmother's old trunk.

"Too Tall Tom can pour the wine," Gypsy Rose said, "and, Dennis, please pull up an extra chair. Rickie's on his way over."

I turned to Jane, marveling at how evenly she filled the

red wineglasses. "Peggy Malfa met me at Barrymore's right after the rehearsal. She's all bent out of shape, really upset that you'd been prying into her past." Jane nodded, looking satisfied. "So tell us, what did you find out about her?"

Placing a glass of wine next to each plate, she said, "Why don't you all sit down?"

Dennis took the chair next to mine. How could he look so crisp and smell so clean this late in the day? I felt like a bag of rags and I didn't want to contemplate what I smelled like.

Even Gypsy Rose laid down her ladle and joined us at the table. Jane had our undivided attention.

"Well, Jake, as you'd pointed out, Peggy Malfa, along with Morgan Drake, and Cynthia Malone, seemed to have landed on Broadway minus a past. Peggy's *Playbill* biography listed no hometown, thanked no family members, gave no college. The blurb began with her New York credits, starting with her first appearance just over ten years ago, in an Off-off Broadway production of *Once Upon a Mattress*. The Carol Burnett role. So she must have been good. But where had she started out? Where had she studied?"

"Right!" I said. "And why all the mystery?"

Jane favored us with one of her annoying cat-that-swallowed-the-canary smiles, and continued. "A cousin of mine had been a stagehand in that production. I stopped by to see him last night."

Gypsy Rose said, "And he remembered Peggy?"

"Oh, yes!" Jane sipped her wine. "Apparently she'd been drinking too much even back then. Rafe told me that he and Peggy had often closed McSorley's."

"Your cousin's name is Rafe?" Modesty sounded surprised. "Rather exotic, isn't it, for such a sensible family?"

"Why would you think that my family . . ." Jane changed her response midsentence. "Do you want to hear about Peggy or not?"

"Yes, of course," Modesty said.

"Then stay on track!"

I asked, "What did Peggy tell Rafe during their late nights together at McSorley's?"

"That she grew up in central Florida. Her father had been a farmer till he died of pancreatic cancer, complicated by decades of heavy boozing, when Peggy was about thirteen. Her mother sold the farm, and they moved to Miami, where Mama bought a condo with the proceeds, and became a working girl. Actually brought the johns home. Peggy led a miserable life, ran away from home several times, and said that when her mother died on her eighteenth birthday, she felt relieved. Legally, she was an adult. And her mother's only heir. Not that there was much money, just enough to get out of Miami. Then, going through some papers, Peggy discovered that she'd been adopted from an orphanage in New York State. She'd been about three, had no memory of the place, but had been delighted to learn those two losers hadn't been her real parents.

"So she sold the condo and moved to Manhattan. One of the reasons that she came to New York was to try and trace her birth mother. Another was to go on the stage. But after she'd been accepted into the American Academy of Dramatic Arts, and became an actress, Peggy told Rafe she gave up the search for her real family."

Too Tall Tom twirled his glass. "But who's to say Peggy hadn't resumed her search again!"

Gypsy Rose said, "Sebastian James's in-laws and his little daughter vanished, you know. They'd left England after his ex-wife committed suicide. As far as I know, no one ever heard from them again."

"This is just too weird," Modesty said. "I spent all day on the computer, hooked up to the Mormon library's awesome research database in Utah, trying to dig up some background on Morgan Drake. Would you believe she'd been dropped off at a Catholic orphanage by her babysitter when both her parents were killed in a car crash?"

I asked, "When did that happen, Modesty? How did you find out her family's real name?"

"I didn't. I typed in 'Morgan Drake' and the dates 1967 to 1972, a five-year range, then searched tons of records, stuff like birth certificates and death certificates. Lots of Drakes, but only one with a child named Morgan. Her parents died in 1971. And I discovered that Morgan was baptized in 1969."

Dennis, who'd been very quiet, asked, "Where was she born?"

"That's the strange thing. I couldn't locate any record of Morgan's birth certificate. Or of her parents' marriage certificate." Modesty reached into her bag and pulled out several pages of notes. "Yes, I found her parents' death certificates. And Morgan's baptismal certificate. St. Mark's Episcopal Church, September 17, 1969. Hastings-on-Hudson. Westchester, New York."

Jane shouted, "Westchester! Peggy Malfa's parents adopted her from an orphanage located in that very same county!"

Before anyone had a chance to react, Modesty jumped back in, stepping on Jane's last line. "But the really intriguing research wasn't delving into Morgan's past. I also phoned another writer who'd attended that Gothic Romance Conference in New Jersey to check out Cynthia Malone. Her story about being adopted from an orphanage in Great Britain is total bull. Sebastian James isn't her father. Cynthia was born in Montefiore Hospital."

"Here in New York City?"

"Yes, Jake, a hometown honey. She was graduated from Christopher Columbus High School in the Bronx, where, according to the yearbook, Cynthia starred in the senior class play. I visited with her guidance counselor this afternoon. An old lady named Mrs. Parker, getting ready to retire, but sharp, remembered Cynthia very well. Said she'd gone on to Parson's for a year, but dropped out. Worked in Macy's, doing alterations. Moved up to window designer. As the *Playbill* indicates, her first

Broadway show was only two years ago. Her mother, née Mary Kelly, died when Cynthia was two, but her father is alive and well, and working as a mechanic at LaGuardia Airport."

I said, "But that's totally nuts. Why would Cynthia make up such a wild story?" Then I thought about the bizarre lunch hour I'd spent with her.

Modesty shrugged. "There's no question that Cynthia's crazy. Like those old ladies in *Arsenic and Old Lace*. Delusional. Didn't like her lower middle class background, so she rewrote it, creating a fantasy about a famous stage star being her father. Then she wormed her way into his life. My money's on Malone. I think she's crazy enough to be our killer."

Twenty-seven

Dennis walked me home. Though only a block away, it felt like a mile. A small child could have comfortably fit in the space between us. Neither the clear night air with a sky full of stars, nor the laughter coming from late diners seated in the open area of the café we passed by, elevated my mood.

At my front door, I hesitated, then asked, "Do you want to come up?" Suspecting that Mom wouldn't be back from Gracie Mansion before midnight, maybe I wanted to talk. Maybe I wanted more.

"No." He brushed a strand of hair away from my eyes. "I think the time for talking is over, Jake." Totally eerie, how well this man read me. "It's decision time. We both know it, don't we? What you may not know is that I won't wait forever." He kissed the top of my head, then turned and walked toward his father's store on Madison.

Home alone. Well, back to plan A. I'd run downstairs to the basement and take a peek in Grandmother O'Hara's old trunk.

The key into the co-op's lobby also opened the door to the basement. I switched on the light at the top of the stairs and the door banged shut behind me. Navigating my way down the steep cement steps, I held on to the banister. Once on the ground, I stared at the neatly numbered walk-in lockers lined up in two rows on both sides of the basement. We had number 201, the same as our apartment. Knowing and trusting all our neighbors, we never bothered to lock it.

Even in the relatively dim light, I had no trouble locating our locker. My old red Schwin bike lay against the chicken-coop-style netting, right next to the padlock. The O'Hara family trunk abutted the Foley family trunk. Except for those three items, the locker was empty. Maura Foley O'Hara had never been a pack rat. I couldn't say the same for the lockers on either side of ours. Their junk piles stretched straight up to the ceiling.

I pulled the cord dangling from the solitary bulb, lighting the cagelike space. Then, from the basket on my bike, I retrieved trunk keys that were attached to tags marked *O'Hara* and *Foley*. Mom's security system.

Feeling nostalgic, I thought about opening Nana Foley's trunk, too. While I'd never known my paternal grandmother, I fondly remembered the warm fuzzy days in Jackson Heights with my maternal grandmother. Time constraints stopped me. If I veered from my mission, I'd be in the basement, mired in memories, for hours.

I lifted the lid, wondering what I'd find and how it could possibly solve my problem. Yellowed tissue paper covered a dress. I gently unwrapped it. A satin wedding gown, almost as yellow as the paper. I caressed the fabric, then held the dress up in front of me, wishing for a mirror, tempted to try it on.

Laying the gown on top of the Foley trunk, I continued to rummage through the O'Hara trunk. Lifting the family Bible, I found a large, black leather diary. On the page dated October 1, 1917, a photograph accompanied the neat penmanship. Granny O'Hara, née Rosemary Reilly, stood in front of an ambulance next to a young man who looked uncannily like Ernest Hemingway. The entry indicated that my grandmother had served with the Red Cross during WWI! How come I'd never known that? Fascinated, I sat on the edge of the Foley trunk and read about my other grandmother's adventures.

Then, stuffing the diary in my tote bag, I kept on digging. Wrapped in a flapper-style silk chemise, I discovered a thick, tarnished brass frame. Missing its glass, the frame held a very faded newspaper clipping from the New York *Herald*, dated May 18, 1919—a picture of the White House, with three women standing in the forefront. The text identified them from left to right as Susan B. Anthony, Victoria Woodhull, and Rosemary Reilly. Jeez! Granny O'Hara had been a suffragette! Had she, like Forrest Gump and Zelig, mysteriously turned up at important historical events? The frame went in my tote bag, too.

I draped the wedding gown over my left arm, turned off the light in the locker, then with my bag—crammed with those precious remnants of Rosemary Reilly O'Hara's past—slung over my shoulder and hugging my chest, I climbed the stairs to the lobby, and shoved open the heavy door.

The tote bag took the bullet.

As I tumbled back down the steps, I heard Mrs. McMahon scream, "Jake!" then the sounds of a scuffle. Landing in a heap on the concrete floor, I heard a crack, then felt a sharp pain in my left ankle. I yanked the tote bag off my shoulder, and scrambled around inside it for my cell phone. I felt the bullet hole in the picture frame.

Dialing 911, I tried to stand. The pain shot up my leg. Pressing the cell phone to my left ear, I reached for the banister with my right hand, and dragged myself up the steps.

The 911 operator answered as I crawled through the door. Whatever I expected to see when I reached the lobby, I could never have conjured up this. As I was giving my name and address, explaining that someone had just shot at me, I spotted Mrs. McMahon pointing a gun in my direction.

She shouted, "Jake, thank God, I thought I'd killed you!"

Had I entered the twilight zone? My elderly neighbor, a dedicated busybody, was basically harmless. Tonight, dressed in her purple polka-dot pajamas and wearing a hair net over her multicolored curlers, she looked more like a clown than a killer.

When I finished giving the information to the operator, I said, "Since the police will be here in a couple of minutes, Mrs. McMahon, you might want to drop that gun."

Her eyes moved from me to the tiny pearl-handled revolver clutched in her right hand. A mixture of dread and disgust filled her fleshy face, then her entire body started to shake. "Don't you see, Jake, if you'd died, I would have been responsible." The gun slid from her hand to the marble floor. Then she sobbed uncontrollably.

I couldn't crawl any farther. She knelt and put her arm around my shoulder.

"We're both okay now, Mrs. M. Why don't you tell me what happened?"

"I had the ten o'clock news on. It was almost over when I heard the front door open, but before I could check out who'd come home, my intercom buzzed."

Mrs. McMahon had to be totally freaked out, to admit that she spied on her neighbors comings and goings!

"I couldn't imagine who would be bothering me so late at night, but I answered."

As if she would ever not answer a buzzer or a doorbell.

"And it was you, Jake. At least she claimed to be you— I thought you sounded hoarse, but I let you—er—her in."

"I was in the basement."

"Yes, she must have been right behind you, and then buzzed me as soon as you went downstairs."

If someone had been on my tail, she could have watched through one of the glass panes in the front door as I'd opened the cellar door. "What happened then?"

"Well, I came out in the hall to check up on you, but there was no one there. I waited a few minutes, then went back into my apartment."

"Maybe the woman had ducked into the elevator when she saw your door start to open."

"I guess that's possible." Mrs. McMahon hung her head. She and I both knew that her spying usually produced better results. "But I stayed by my front door. Then, about ten minutes later, I heard some noise. I stepped out into the hall, just as that woman shot you!"

"My God! What did you do?" Guilt swept over me. "She could have shot you, too!"

"When you fell down the basement steps, I thought she'd killed you. I screamed, then rammed her rear end, knocking her to the floor. Her blonde wig went flying!" Mrs. McMahon gestured to a mass of brassy curls on the floor near the elevator door. "She dropped the gun. I grabbed it. In what seemed like a split second, she jumped up, spun around, and ran out the front door. I wanted to shoot her, Jake, but I couldn't stop shaking! Then, like the ghost of Christmas Past, you appeared. I'd been so sure that you were dead. How could I ever have told your mother?"

As the sirens heralded the police's arrival, I kissed Mrs. McMahon's wrinkled cheek. "My mother and I thank you!"

Twenty-eight

Since my attempted murder had taken place in the Nineteenth Precinct, Ben Rubin and Sandy Ellis arrived on the scene shortly after the uniforms.

They found me sitting on the floor next to the wig, leaning against the wall. My entire body ached, my ankle throbbed, and I felt faint.

Ben took one look at me and carried me to his car.

"Where are we going?" I wrapped my arms around his neck, my tote bag, now containing evidence, still dangled from my shoulder, flapping against his right side.

"Mount Sinai. I don't want to wait for an ambulance. You look like hell and I think your ankle's broken." He bent down, staring at me intently, a sudden smile lighting up his grim face. "And, since you'll be getting X rays, I'll suggest they take a few of your brain."

He pushed the front passenger seat all the way back, so my leg stuck straight out in front of me, then turned the siren on full blast. We arrived at the hospital on 103rd and Fifth in just under two minutes.

Thinking that I might pass out from the pain in my

leg—and, though I'd never tell Ben, my head hurt, too—I insisted on making a statement.

"Either Cynthia Malone, Peggy Malfa, or Morgan Drake has to be the shooter. Make sure that Mulroney and you check out their alibis, Ben. One of those women killed Elaine Eden and Tristan Hunter."

"You shouldn't be talking."

"No! You listen to me. Talk to Modesty, Jane, and Too Tall Tom. The ghosts can fill you in on each woman's background. Then, when Mrs. McMahon gives Sandy Ellis the description of the shooter, remember that all three of them can look very much alike. Nondescript brown wrens if they so choose. But capable of becoming very beautiful butterflies. You're dealing with two actresses and a makeup artist here. All mistresses of disguise. Actually, Cynthia Malone used to be an actress, too. She starred in her high school play. Remind Mulroney that a young woman had been spotted in the Leo House lobby just before Tristan's murder."

The last thing I heard before I passed out was Ben's groan.

· · · · ·

I awoke on a gurney in the Mount Sinai emergency room, but before the doctor could set my ankle, he had to contend with Gypsy Rose, Aaron, Mom, and Dennis, who was holding my hand. Mom must have called him. Over my strenuous objections, they were all insisting that I stay overnight. The surgeon, describing my injury as a simple fracture that would necessitate wearing a cast for six damn weeks, administered painkillers, then admitted me.

Gypsy Rose, after stacking my hospital room's bedside table with every possible contingency, and Mom and Aaron, totally exhausted, finally went home around two on Wednesday morning. Dennis lingered behind just long enough to give me a good-night kiss.

I slept like the dead.

At 6:00 A.M.—without offering me as much as a glass of water—a relentlessly cheerful nurse drew blood, then wheeled me down to radiology, where a technician took X rays of every inch of my anatomy.

By 9:00 A.M., sunlight streamed through the window in my hospital room. I was back in bed, my left leg propped high on pillows, following a sponge bath and finally getting to brush my teeth, enjoying a cup of tea.

Sitting in the chair to my right, not as a visitor, but in his professional capacity as Chief of Homicide at the Nineteenth Precinct, Ben Rubin was taking my official statement.

I gestured to the crutches lying across the bottom of the bed. "Want to see how I can navigate with these? I had a lesson this morning and I think—with practice— I'll be able to make it down the aisle on Friday night."

Ben glanced at his watch. "Let's try and finish this."

"Right." No good-morning kiss from him, and he hadn't as yet cracked a smile.

"So, since you never actually saw this other woman, you aren't a witness."

"Yes, I guess that's true . . . but—"

"And we only have Mrs. McMahon's word that a second woman was with her in the lobby."

"Jesus, Ben! What are you saying? You can't believe that Mrs. McMahon shot me!"

"No, I don't, but lacking evidence to the contrary, Lt. Mulroney might. And I doubt he'll buy into your three women theory."

"Do you?" Anger rose like bile in my throat.

He finally smiled. Crooked, rueful, but definitely a smile. "Well, when we finish here, I'm going over to Modesty's to hear what the ghosts have learned about the ladies in question. She has a pile of computer printouts ready for me. Then if the gun is registered—"

"What about that wig? Doesn't that prove the killer wore a disguise?"

"Or Mrs. McMahon might have been playing dress up.

Try to see this from a cop's point of view. You're convinced that one of those women is our killer. And that the shooting has to be connected to Elaine's and Tristan's murders. Mulroney may not see it that way."

"Did you at least check out their alibis?"

"Jake, I'm on your side. I went back to work as soon as I left the emergency room last night, and spent most of the night interviewing all three of them. I still haven't been to bed."

I noticed the dark shadows under his eyes and the growth of stubble on his chin. Feeling like a selfish fool, I said, "I'm sorry."

He patted my hand.

"So what did you find out?"

"You segue from saying sorry to hurry-up-and-tell-me-everything without missing a beat."

I didn't even try to deny his accusation. I just smiled and waited.

He shook his head. "None of them has a real alibi, but each has a quasi-alibi."

"What does that mean?"

"Well, I caught up with Peggy Malfa about seven this morning. Woke her up. The lady was very hungover and very annoyed. She told me she'd spent the evening at the Marriott Marquis with some Texan she picked up at Barrymore's. Said you'd met him, too."

"Much earlier—six or so—around the time I'd talked to you on the phone. When I returned to the bar, she and he were chatting. Then I went up to Gypsy Rose's. Peggy was still with him at the hotel at eleven last night?"

"She told me that he'd passed out cold around eleven-thirty, so she got dressed and went home. Her doorman said she came in a little before midnight. However, I couldn't find anyone at the hotel who'd seen her leave. I spoke to Tex an hour ago. He hasn't a clue about what time he passed out and he certainly has 'no recollection of when the little lady left.' "

"If she did leave the hotel by ten-thirty, she could have been in Carnegie Hill by eleven."

"Right. As could Cynthia Malone."

"She's a strange one, Ben. What's her quasi-alibi?"

"Went out for some special cat food at about ten-fifteen. The clerk at the open-all-night supermarket had bagged her catnip at about ten-thirty. Cynthia told me she went straight home—'my babies need me'—but no one could confirm that."

"Maybe she grabbed a cab up to Carnegie Hill, took a shot at me, and fed the cats a midnight supper."

"Or it might have been lady number three."

"Morgan Drake."

"Her story is the best of the bunch. Lt. Mulroney released Philip Knight at seven-thirty last night. Morgan picked him up and they celebrated over dinner at Alain Ducasse's fancy French restaurant in the Essex House."

"Some celebration! That's the place with a padded footstool for every lady's purse."

"Dined there with Dennis, I presume." Frost coated his words.

As the blood rushed to my face, I pretended to fuss with the sheets, then gave a small nod.

He emitted something between a chuckle and a snort, then continued. "They left the restaurant before ten and, supposedly, arrived at Philip's apartment on Fifth Avenue and Seventy-eighth Street—the huge one that he'd shared with Elaine Eden—around ten-fifteen, and were in bed by ten-thirty."

"Then Morgan's alibi isn't quasi?"

"It is to me. She slept in the guest bedroom, two thousand square feet away from Philip's."

The same nurse who'd given me the sponge bath came in, followed by Mom and Gypsy Rose.

"All of your tests turned out okay, Ms. O'Hara. The doctor says you're out of here. I'll get the wheelchair."

My mother's eyes were red and weepy, but smiling

through those tears, she said, "Thank God you're okay, darling!"

Gypsy Rose, holding a huge bouquet of white flowers, gave me a big kiss.

Mom perched on the edge of my bed. "Sandy Ellis returned your tote bag, except for the frame with the bullet hole. I've been reading my former mother-in-law's diary. Jake, do you know that your grandmother slept with Ernest Hemingway?"

Twenty-nine

Some detective I am.

The hospital routine had kept me very busy. And, since Gypsy Rose had stockpiled a complete care package on my bedside table—toothbrush, toothpaste, comb, brush, tissues, cold cream, moisturizer, and even cotton swabs—I never missed my tote bag.

Now the police had pawed through it and Mom, beating me to the punch, had read the diary.

Though I felt my paternal grandmother's privacy had been seriously invaded by my mother, I wanted to spend the rest of the day in bed, with Rosemary Reilly O'Hara's diary as my only companion.

No such luck. I had four phone messages, three of them indicating that the caller absolutely had to see me.

Cynthia Malone's was the most intriguing.

"Jake, I must explain what happened during Elaine Eden's final bourbon and bonbon binge. I understand you've been injured, but have been released from hospital. May I come to call around three this afternoon?"

Once again I wondered how a kid could grow up in the Bronx and sound like British royalty.

Auturo Como's message never mentioned the shooting, not even as obliquely as Cynthia's had. He wanted to drop off his suggestions for any last-minute script changes after today's rehearsal. They'd be quitting early, so that the cast could grab some rest before tonight's dress rehearsal.

And, of all people, Philip Knight wanted a "private word" with me. He didn't say what that word might be.

The fourth message was from Ben, who would not be stopping by, but would be sending Sandy Ellis. To baby-sit, I presumed. I'd bet that Mom, Aaron, Gypsy Rose, Ben, and, probably, Dennis had decided I should have police protection.

I left four messages, asking all of my potential visitors to come at three.

Then, exhausted but filled with glee, I fell asleep.

．．．．．

The smell of Gypsy Rose's chicken soup wakened me around one.

And I needed to get to the bathroom. My crutches were on the chair next to the bed. I made a lunge for them, then tumbled onto the floor, landing on my fanny, legs spread out in a V, the left one in the cast under the bed.

Wasn't this going to be a fun recovery period?

"Mom!" I screamed. "Gypsy Rose!"

Gypsy Rose came dashing through the door. "Oh God, darling, let me help you up."

Between us, I managed to get to the bathroom. Everything in slow motion. Jeez! Six weeks of this!

"Where's Mom?"

"At the grocery store. I'm in charge here. Flowers have been arriving every half hour. Dennis. Ben. Too Tall Tom. Modesty and Rickie. Jane sent a vase from Tiffany filled with dried herbs."

I smiled.

"Now, would you rather have a tray in here or do you want to come to the kitchen?"

I'd have preferred to squirrel into bed for the duration, but I hobbled to the table.

Watching Gypsy Rose pour the soup and butter the homemade muffins, I thought about how much she loved Mom and me, how good and generous she'd been to us all these years, and how much she'd miss Mom. They were closer than most sisters. All this time I'd been feeling sorry for myself. In many ways, Mom's marriage must be even more devastating for her best friend. While I couldn't take Mom's place, I could be available for Gypsy Rose.

"So, who's minding the store?" I didn't want Gypsy Rose to neglect her business.

"Christian Holmes and the two part-timers. Don't worry, Jake, I've got it covered. And we're closing on Friday for the wedding. Now finish your soup, then we'll practice walking on those suckers."

After lunch, she put on Mom's favorite Fred Astaire singing Cole Porter CD, and I started moving.

By 2:30, I had performed for Mom, making U-turns on my crutches, put on my makeup, slipped into a new sweatshirt, slit the left leg on a pair of old loose chinos, and laced up the right sneaker. Ready to greet my visitors.

Like Noah's Ark, they came in pairs. Sandy Ellis and Philip Knight arrived at 2:55 and rode up in the elevator together, surprised to learn they were both going to the same co-op.

The living room looked and smelled like a funeral parlor.

As Gypsy Rose served tea and cookies, I greeted the other two guests, savoring the irony of Cynthia Malone arriving with the man who thought she'd killed his fiancée, Philip Knight.

"A gathering of suspects?" Auturo asked, checking out Sandy's long legs.

"No," I said, "this is Detective Ellis from the Nineteenth Precinct's Homicide Department. She's not a suspect." I watched a small grin quickly form, then fade on Sandy's lips.

When they all, even Auturo, had accepted a cup of tea and had been properly introduced to Mom and Gypsy Rose—who then excused themselves—I turned to Cynthia, probably the weakest link. "You wanted to explain Elaine Eden's last binge to me?"

Philip started, but then sat back, crossing one slim leg over the other. A move I wouldn't be making till Christmas.

In a Perry Mason moment, Cynthia said, "Yes. I do want to explain. This may look bad for me, but"—she jerked her thumb at Philip—"he knows the truth about what happened, and that's why he's telling everyone that I killed her."

I said, "This was after the scene in Barrymore's, right?" She nodded. "Well, what did happen?"

"After I got Sebastian out of there, I went back to the theater to work on Elaine's costume. About thirty minutes later, Elaine and Philip showed up. She was in a rage. The jumpsuit was all wrong. My measurements were all wrong. I'd made her look all out of proportion. She felt frumpy wearing it. My beautiful creation. I screamed that her shape was all wrong, that her body was out of proportion, not my design."

Auturo growled, "I never heard about this . . ."

I shot him a dirty look. "Go on, Cynthia," I said, not wanting to interrupt her flow.

"Finally, Elaine calmed down, and I agreed to fix the costume. Philip Knight told her to call him when we finished and he'd send a limo to bring her home. That's when she really lost it. Screamed that the jumpsuit would look better on Morgan, wouldn't it? Said that she knew Philip wanted to get rid of her, that he thought she was over the hill, that he wanted Morgan to play Suzy Q. She even accused him of having an affair with Morgan!"

I glanced at Philip. He bit his lip, but otherwise remained stoic.

"After Knight had gone, Elaine ripped open a five-pound box of bonbons and brought out the bourbon. For every seam I let out, she seemed to wolf down a pound of candy and a jelly glass of booze. Frankly, I'd hoped she eat and drink herself to death. But she didn't die till the next day."

I turned to Philip. "Tell us again, why was Morgan Drake wearing a red jumpsuit on Saturday? Ready to leap into the starring role, wasn't she?"

Of course I knew the rationale. Peggy had shown up drunk one time too many that morning, and Morgan, who knew all of Elaine's lines as well as her own, was asked to understudy the understudy. Then, according to Cynthia, Philip had told Morgan she'd play the Suzy Q role on opening night. I wanted to see if I could make him squirm.

Not a chance.

"I think you know the answer to that, Jake." Philip sounded as suave as he looked. Unruffled by Cynthia or by me. I'd bet Lt. Mulroney hadn't made him squirm either.

Auturo Como, if not actually squirming, looked damn uncomfortable. Sweat beaded his fleshy face. He used one of Mom's best napkins to wipe it away.

Philip stood, then crossed the room to stand next to me. Sandy Ellis, in full alert mode, followed his every move.

He shook his long index finger at me. "Why did I bother coming here? You're a very pushy young woman, Jake O'Hara. I'd hoped your nosy streak might lead you to the killer, but alas, I see that you're too thick. And yes, for the record, I do believe that Cynthia, completely obsessed with Sebastian James, killed Elaine."

"You want us to believe you believe that, but I don't."

He lunged toward me.

"Easy, Mr. Knight." Sandy Ellis's words sounded like sugarcoated steel.

Philip laughed. "Jake, are you suffering from the same

delusion as Lt. Mulroney? Even though he released me last night, the man is convinced I'm guilty. I admit I wanted to get rid of Elaine."

Auturo jumped up, probably picturing his director being hauled off to Riker's and *Suzy Q* closing before it opened.

Sandy Ellis, still using that odd blend of sugar and steel said, "Sit down, Mr. Como."

He did, and the smooth Mr. Knight picked up his tale. "Though I wanted Elaine out of the show, I didn't shout it from the rafters as Gareth and Auturo did. They even took out an insurance policy, no doubt planning to make sure that she wouldn't be the star on opening night."

Auturo again started to get up, caught Sandy's eye, and sat back down.

Philip, ignoring Auturo, continued. "That's why I'd told Morgan she'd have the lead on opening night. I felt certain that Selby-Steed and Como would find a way to get rid of Elaine. Look, for both personal and professional reasons, I did want Morgan Drake to play Suzy Q, but I didn't kill Elaine." He spun around, now pointing his finger at Cynthia. "This woman murdered my fiancée!"

I nudged his backside with my crutch. "Philip, why don't you tell us who killed Tristan?"

When he turned back to me, he appeared to have aged ten years.

I kept going. "You're afraid that someone else murdered him, aren't you? That's why when I ran the two killer theory by you in the theater the other day, you recoiled. You've been trying to pin this on Cynthia from day one. It's okay for a wardrobe mistress to be a murderer—even a double murderer—she's not indispensable; however, if your star is arrested for murder, *Suzy Q* will close. What a sterling character you are, Philip. You're sure that Sebastian James killed Tristan, but you'd be delighted to let Cynthia Malone take the rap, if it would save the show."

As they all stared at me, I delivered my exit line. "I assure you, Mr. Knight, there's only one killer. Now, if you'll excuse me, I need to get some rest. I wouldn't want to miss opening night."

Thirty

On Thursday morning, I didn't wake up until almost eleven. My leg hurt like hell. Mom had left water and Advil on my bedside table. I took two.

Last night I'd turned off both my phones, sent Sandy Ellis back to Homicide, kissed Mom and Gypsy Rose good night, and went to bed with Rosemary Reilly O'Hara's diary.

Granny hadn't turned up in quite as many places as *Zelig*, but she had a hell of a life, including as Mom had noted, a hot romance with a very young Hemingway on and off the battlefields during WWI. Of course, Rosemary Reilly had only been nineteen herself.

Unlike the rest of my family, my paternal grandmother hadn't been a native New Yorker. She'd grown up in Boston and came to Manhattan at seventeen to study nursing. When America had finally entered the war in 1917, Rosemary joined the Red Cross and, a week later, sailed to Europe. Since she'd been assigned to a hospital in Italy, I wondered if she could have been the true inspiration for the Catherine character in *A Farewell to Arms*!

After the affair and the war were over, Granny came

home and joined the Women's Suffrage Movement. A real rabble-rouser, she'd been arrested no less than four times. When the women got the vote, Granny switched gears, and worked as an extra in silent pictures in a Long Island City movie studio. Though she never actually penned it, I suspected that she had a romance with John Gilbert. He'd been featured in over thirty pages of the diary.

By June of 1931, still single at thirty-three, she was running a fledging radio station in Brooklyn. That's where she met and married my grandfather, John O'Hara, a handsome New York City fireman, five years younger than she. My father, born seven months later, weighed in at eight pounds, three ounces—far too big a baby to be premature.

Granny quit her job, raised her son, read three books a week, completed the Sunday *Times* crossword puzzle in ink, and espoused the ACLU's causes, much to my conservative grandfather's horror.

She died of a heart attack at forty-four, in the middle of a march on City Hall, protesting against lower pay for female city employees. My father, her only child, was ten.

God, how I wished I had known her!

This morning, it occurred to me that I'd never lived away from home and, other than delving into murder cases that had landed both Mom and me in the hospital, my life experience has been very parochial.

It also occurred to me that, at thirty-four, I might be ready to change.

Switch gears. Spend some time alone with Jake. Make a difference to the world at large and to myself in particular. At least finish the damn Sunday *Times* puzzle!

After a noonish breakfast/lunch with Mom and Gypsy Rose, and a long struggle to get washed and dressed, I turned the phones back on.

Several members of Ghostwriters Anonymous had called, including Too Tall Tom, Jane, and Modesty—all wanting to know if I'd be attending *Suzy Q*'s opening and would I be okay for the wedding. Dennis had called twice. Said he had news for me. Ben wanted me to get back to him at once. Mr. Kim was sending a basket of fruit. Auturo Como, skipping any niceties, said last night's dress rehearsal stunk and he wanted more rewrites. Mrs. Mc-Mahon, using her most funereal voice, told me again how very, very sorry she was.

Where to start?

I punched Dennis's number.

"I'm going to live."

"Jake! I hope you didn't lose all feeling in your left foot. I know your toes are the center of your sexual desire."

"Very funny. What did you want to tell me?"

"Hey, I hinted to an editor at Pax Publishers that a previously undiscovered murder mystery by Zelda Fitzgerald may be coming into my possession. He jumped at it. So could you hurry up and ghostwrite the first chapter and a brief synopsis? We're looking at high six figures here."

My God. I'd be a woman of independent means! Maybe I could buy the co-op upstairs! Independent or not, I wouldn't want to leave Carnegie Hill. If I had enough money, I could live on my own, but still be near Mom and Gypsy Rose.

"I'll start tomorrow."

"And have it finished by next Friday?"

"Well, Gypsy Rose will have to channel Zelda, then—"

"Yeah, I guess ghosting for a ghost may present some challenges, but you'll handle them. I'll set up an appointment with the editor. I'm picking you ladies up tonight. See you later."

I moved on to Ben.

"Jake, I want you to know that Mulroney's not adverse to your three women—one killer—theory, but he's scrounging around for hard evidence."

"What about the gun?"

"Not registered. No prints. They're looking for DNA,

but those tests take a while. Mulroney's on top of it."

"Good."

"Can I talk you out of going to the opening?"

"No. Mom and Gypsy Rose are looking forward to it. Aaron, too. We all are. And, I may have to work tonight. I have to call Auturo back. He sounded stressed. Big time."

"If you're right, one of those women attempted to murder you. So watch your step." He chuckled. "Well, you know . . . don't play Nancy Drew."

When I reached Auturo, he begged me to sit backstage and rewrite throughout the entire show. "Your lines have bite, Jake. I marked up three bland spots in act one. Can you come early and make those changes? If the critics like act one, we have a shot. You know the screenwriters on *Casablanca* made up the dialogue as they went along. Is this so different? And, there really aren't all that many changes in act two or three."

I'll bet.

By the time I'd returned all the calls and listened to my dear friends' condolences and good wishes, it was time to get dressed for the opening.

I made one last call, leaving a message for Dennis, asking him to pick us up an hour earlier.

Mom and Gypsy Rose had put together an outfit for me. Mom's blackwatch plaid, very full taffeta skirt, which she'd only worn once last Christmas, and that completely covered my cast, Gypsy Rose's black velvet riding jacket—"It's way too small for me, Jake, but it will be perfect on you"—a three-strand pearl necklace that Mom said had once belonged to my paternal grandmother, and a black satin flat for my right foot.

I said, "I love the way the pearls look against the black velvet."

"You look lovely, darling." My mother picked up her makeup case. "Can you do something with her hair, Gypsy Rose?"

As Mom was applying blush, murder crossed my mind.

Though I might be heading for major changes and a new way of living, I had one more case to solve. And I was missing something. Something Modesty had said about the results of her research into the three suspects' backgrounds. Or something she hadn't said . . .

"Sit still, Jake!" My mother sounded frustrated.

"Are we almost done? I have to call Modesty."

The buzzer interrupted me. Dennis had arrived.

I stuffed my cell phone into my tiny satin purse. I'd call her from the theater.

Thirty-one

Even though we arrived an hour ahead of curtain, limousines were circling the Baronet like wagon trains. Glamour was in high gear. *Suzy Q*, completely sold out, had attracted a broad spectrum of first-nighters, ranging from movie stars to former presidents.

I had three tickets for Mom, Gypsy Rose, and Aaron, only because Dennis had written those seventh row center seats into my contract. Since I'd be working in the wings all night, I wondered if Auturo had sold my seat.

I couldn't get over how well my mother had handled the attempted murder of her dearly beloved daughter. While pleased that she hadn't carried on, hovering incessantly, and insisting that I stay home under lock and key, a small part of me resented her apparently sanguine approach to my near-death experience.

Both she and Gypsy Rose, probably for my benefit, were putting up a brave front. And their best faces forward. They looked great. So did Aaron in his well-tailored tuxedo. The same one he'd be getting married in tomorrow night!

As the usher showed them to their seats, I kissed Mom

and Gypsy Rose, full of gratitude for all their love and support. Then I went backstage.

. . . . .

Peggy Malfa, wearing the red jumpsuit and full stage makeup, looking so like Morgan Drake that I'd thought she was, grabbed my arm. "Are you okay?" Before I could answer, she said, "Why does that cop Mulroney think I tried to kill you? What did you tell him about me?"

I decided it was show time.

"Tell me about the locket, Peggy."

All the makeup on Broadway couldn't have hidden her flush. "What locket?"

"The one you accused Morgan of stealing. You never had a locket, did you, Peggy? You just wanted Morgan to look bad. Isn't that why you lied? Why you searched Morgan's dressing room? All part of your act, wasn't it?"

"You bitch! Is that what you told Mulroney?"

"Not yet."

"It's too bad that bullet missed you!" She stomped off.

Auturo came up behind me, "What's with that broad?"

He handed me a script, then led me to an armchair with an ottoman, just off stage right. "Sit. You'll be comfortable here and you can see most of the action and hear every line. Not that you'd want to hear some of them."

"I'll do the act one changes now."

"Yeah. Hurry up. They're all Suzy Q's lines. I want to give them to Morgan before curtain."

I glanced at my watch. "That's only fifty minutes away."

Auturo grinned. A sadist's grin. "She's a quick study."

While the stagehands, swiftly and silently, were moving scenery and props, working their magic, creating the courtyard in Katmandu, and Cynthia Malone was hustling from one chore to another, fetching and carrying for Morgan Drake, I made the changes. Then, just before the orchestra began the overture, Auturo collected them. How I wished I could see the expression on Morgan's face when he delivered those new lines to her dressing room.

With nothing to do for the moment, that mysterious something, that missing piece—or whatever—from Modesty's search, caught my attention again.

One of these three women had to be the daughter Sebastian James had abandoned. The daughter whose mother had committed suicide. The daughter determined to take revenge, by killing Elaine, the woman who'd stolen her father. Then killing Tristan, the stepbrother she'd never known, but who'd lived with her father, while she'd never seen him again.

God! Could Sebastian be next?

I pulled out my cell phone and called Modesty.

"Hey, can you do me a favor and check out some stuff on your computer."

"Shoot—oh—maybe, under the circumstances, not the right word . . ."

I laughed. "I'm sorry to dump this on you, but I know you have the software . . ."

"Like I said, shoot."

"Okay, our killer is one of the three women. So here goes. Find out who Peggy Malfa's real parents were. How long had she been in that orphanage? And could her biological mother have been British?"

"Got it. What else?"

"How old had Morgan Drake's parents been when they were killed in that car crash? Were their ages on the death certificate?"

"Okay."

"And were Morgan and Peggy really in the same orphanage? They would have been there at different times. But find out."

"What about Cynthia Malone?"

"I don't think she's the one. But we can't forget about her. Just because Philip Knight tried to frame her doesn't mean she's not the killer. So are we certain that the child

born in Montefiore Hospital didn't die? That Cynthia
hadn't been adopted to replace her. A real long shot, but
there might have been a private adoption."

"Or she's just a nut."

"Right!"

"I'll get back to you. May take a while."

"Thanks, Modesty."

· · · · ·

The applause after act one lasted ten minutes.
Sebastian had been sober and sensational. Morgan had
learned her new lines, acted her heart out, and sang like
a nightingale. Unless acts two and three turned out to be
total disasters, Auturo and Gareth had a hit.

Cynthia Malone came over and sat on my ottoman
during intermission. "Thank you for defending me. Philip
Knight is an evil man. I knew straightaway that I'd been
wrong to have said such cruel things to you the other
afternoon. Caesar, Cleopatra, and I would be happy to
have you visit us again."

· · · · ·

A stagehand walked around, yelling, "Act two. One
minute to curtain!" Another shouted, "Places!"

Sir Gareth Selby-Steed laid a hand on my shoulder.
"Going well, don't you think?"

I nodded, but didn't reply. The prospect of all these
miserable people getting rich gnawed at my gut. Hell, if
the play's a hit, I'd be one of those people making pots
of money.

Following an old Broadway tradition, the director
watched the show from the back of the theater, mixing
with the audience at intermission, getting a feel for their
reaction, so I didn't have to put up with Philip Knight.
The composer left me to join the director.

Sebastian took his position on stage. Morgan stood next
to me waiting to go on. I flipped my script open to act

two. It read: *Suzy Q enters from stage right and, mistaking the ambassador for an intruder, shoots him.*

My cell phone, clutched in my hand, rang.

Morgan shifted her small pearl-handled revolver from her left to her right hand and gave me a dirty look as I quickly answered the call.

Modesty said, "Forget about Cynthia. I spoke to her father. He said his daughter wishes she'd been adopted, but she's Italian and Irish, despite pretending to be a British blue blood since Diana married Charles."

"Go on," I whispered.

The curtain rose.

"Peggy was in a totally different orphanage than Morgan. Her biological mother was an unwed teenager from New Rochelle."

"You're amazing!"

"I'm a hacker."

I watched Morgan enter the courtyard on cue. God! Could that gun be loaded with bullets, not blanks?

I grabbed my crutches and stood, juggling the phone.

"Morgan's parents were in their early sixties when they died. They wouldn't have had a kid that young. So they must have been her grandparents. And get this, Morgan's middle name on her baptismal certificate is Catherine. The same name as Sebastian's ex-wife."

Morgan aimed the gun at Sebastian.

I dropped the phone, and hobbled onstage. The audience stirred. Someone gasped. I heard my mother cry out, "Jake!"

At that exact moment, Morgan spun around and pointed her gun at me. I plunged forward, trying to balance on my left crutch, then using my right crutch, I knocked the gun out of her hand.

Sebastian, who had been frozen, finally made a move, scooping up the gun before Morgan could reach it.

I fell on my fanny to the sounds of thunderous applause.